SAVAGE: A NOVEL
By Angel Berry

"The hand of the Lord came upon me and carried me out in the spirit of the Lord and set me down in the midst of the valley and that was full of bones. And He made me pass by them round about, and lo! they were exceedingly many on the surface of the valley, and lo! They were exceedingly dry. Then He said to me, 'Son of man, can these bones become alive?' And I answered, O Lord God, you alone know." – Ezekiel 37:1-3

"Then He said to me, 'Prophesy to the spirit, prophecy, O son of man, and say to the spirit, so says the Lord God: From four sides come, O spirit, breathe into these slain ones that they may live.' " – Ezekiel 37:9

"And they will ask if this is the truth. I will answer in advance: No, this is not the truth. It is only a small part - a tiny fraction of the truth. The essential truth, the real truth, cannot be described even with the most powerful pen." – From the account of Stefan Ernest, *Words to Outlive Us: Eyewitness Accounts from the Warsaw Ghetto*

PROLOGUE

"Wake up!"

Tomas' eyes flew open and his body stiffened instantly in anticipation of a blow. He grunted as the hard, rubber sole of a black boot fell heavily upon his face and smashed his head against the floor nearly crushing his cheekbone. The owner of the boot bent at the hip and stared coldly down at him, deliberately leaning his weight onto Tomas' head before swiftly lifting his foot and bringing it down hard into his ribs, and Tomas doubled over and would have retched had there been anything in his stomach.

He lay there desperately gasping for air while the SS officer stared down at him smugly, calmly, and rocked on the balls of his feet with his hands held firmly behind his back where he grasped the hard, leather handle of a stockwhip. He stood wide-legged, his back ramrod straight, and though he spoke perfect Polish, his German accent was military strict - his tone clipped and harsh.

"Get up and get your shit." He spat impatiently, as if he

had said the words a hundred times before. His handlebar mustache twitched as he spoke and he wore a long leather coat in spite of the warm weather.

Feverish and bewildered, Tomas scrambled to his feet and looked around the room in a pain-filled daze. There were two other SS men in the room - one was a short, middle-aged, blonde-haired man whose eyes darted about nervously as if he waited for someone to bolt from the closet, and the other, a large giant of a man who sported a rifle and a surprisingly calm, understanding look in his eyes.

Tomas braced for impact and his back muscles bunched as he was seized by the collar and flung across the room. There was a solid thud as he hit the wall and his back muscles constricted painfully while his shoulders screamed in agony. His stomach turned weakly and he grimaced as sickness moved through his empty gut.

He heard his sister, Avigail, whimper from the front room and he became frantic, worried that something bad was happening to her, and by aid of the wall, he stumbled dizzily to his feet meaning to run to her, but was hit in the face with the back of a meaty fist. As he fell to the ground, blood gushed from his nose and dripped onto the bare, hardwood floor and ran down the front of his thermal shirt.

The officer came and placed his booted foot onto Tomas' chest and once more leaned his weight down upon him. His eyes were blue granite, and as he leaned over him and their eyes met, thick hatred permeated the air and made Tomas afraid to stir though Avigail's whimpering troubled him greatly. His eyes moved desperately to the doorway of his bedroom and he wondered what was happening to his family.

"Get up and get your shit." The officer spat at him again, emphasizing each word carefully through clenched teeth.

Tomas was grabbed by his collar by the same beefy fist that had moments ago knocked him senseless and yanked roughly to his feet - jerked up with so much force that his head snapped back and he bit his tongue, but he was held there by the collar, as if in a trance, and allowed to regain his balance, and when his eyes came back into focus they met the no-nonsense, patient gaze of his calm restrainer, and was half-carried, half-yanked into the front room where his mother and father stood with his weeping sister.

Miriam's eyes widened when she saw the blood that covered her son and she placed a fist between her teeth to stifle a terrified scream as Gideon reached for him. Tomas staggered to his parents, and as they hugged him, he looked into his father's eyes and saw fear.

"What is it now, Papa?"

"We're being evicted." Gideon told his son quietly, begging Tomas with his eyes to obey for the sake of his sister and mother – so that they would be able to remain together.

As they were violently pushed down the steps of their flat, Avigail gasped with surprise at the long line of people gathered in the street after having been also removed from their homes, and Miriam turned and sharply shushed her.

In this way, at the age of eighteen, Tomas met manhood violently, and as far as he could remember, that is when the night terrors began.

PART ONE

CHAPTER ONE

"The first time I saw him, I knew what he wanted from me. He was not a burden, but he was heavy." Scarlett Ouo, 1955

New York City, 1991

"There is no way that I'm going to be able to stay in bed for the next two months, Amir. There's no way."

Ava lifted her heavy body a few inches from the mattress and shifted to allow her husband to slide a pillow beneath her then turned on her side and gave him her back, not wanting him to see the irritated scowl on her face. Amir held back a laugh and leaned over his wife to place a kiss on her chubby cheek. He truly did hate to see her so uncomfortable, but she was extremely comical in her agitation and he was enjoying her immensely. He slid a hand over her thick midriff and rested it over her large stomach while gently kneading the small of her back. She sighed then and after a few moments relaxed and allowed him to rub the tension from her tired muscles.

"I just wish that this baby would hurry up, Amir. Two

months is so long."

Ava resumed her complaint and Amir did not respond but continued his kneading, rolling his knuckles and the pads of his fingers along her spine and over her shoulder blades.

"I'm so fat." Ava said, kicking at the covers in annoyance.

She turned over on her back then and stared up at him. Her nightgown had twisted about her body and she struggled with it dramatically, lips pouted, skin flushed with the glow of pregnancy, and he could not help but to chuckle at the sight she made.

Amir smiled when Ava cut her eyes and glared at him as if she felt that he was the cause of her distress. He read her mind then and completed her sentence out loud...

"This is all your fault."

...they said in concert, and he smiled down at her lovingly, and against her will, she returned his lazy grin and he leaned over and kissed the tip of her nose.

"Bedrest won't be so bad, sweetheart. I'll get you some crossword puzzles. You can watch movies, sleep." Amir's face lit up as if she were in for the fun of her life. "Time will be up before you know it," he said, raising a tan, slender hand before her eyes and snapping his fingers.

Ava dreamily watched her husband while he leaned over her and spoke. He hadn't shaved in days and dark stubble covered his neck and jawline. His warm, whiskey colored eyes held her own, crinkling slightly in the corners as he teased her, and she reached up and ran a hand over his black, short cropped hair and let her fingers trail slowly down his neck to venture into the thin, wiry hair that covered his broad chest. No matter how much she whined and complained about being pregnant, Ava loved the fact that she was having Amir's baby. Since the day they had met, the only thing she had ever wanted to do in the world was be his wife.

"And you're not fat, Ava. You're plump. Pleasantly plump, dear."

He paused then and watched her seductively nibble at her bottom lip while she flirted with her eyes. He felt shy then, as always, and averted his gaze. Ava had always made him feel this way, and he closed his eyes when she sat up and then moaned when her warm mouth found his own. He cupped her face in his hands and kissed her lips, then her eyes, then her nose again.

"Go to work, Amir." Ava told him, smiling as her fingers moved deftly over his favorite tie – the sapphire blue one – a gift from his mother. After creating the perfect knot, she playfully bit his chin. "I will try my best to carry your elephantine child for two more months," she teased.

He chuckled and pulled her close, squeezing her to him until she began to giggle and protest, then he pecked her once more on the nose before standing up to tuck his shirt into his trousers. His eyes never left her. After he buckled his belt, he leaned over her once more.

"Ava, please listen to the doctor – at least for today. If I find out that you've snuck off to the grocer –"

"I won't go anywhere, Amir."

Ava lay back on the pillows and rolled her eyes skyward though Amir pointed a finger at her in warning. He grabbed his blazer from the bed and shoved his arms into the sleeves.

"If my father calls, ask him to come by for dinner."

"I will." Ava whispered and blew him a kiss.

Ava listened and waited for the front door to close before turning and heaving her body out of bed. With her hands pressed firmly to the small of her back, she slid her feet into an old pair of Amir's slippers then waddled awkwardly to the bathroom. When she reached the sink, she held on to it tightly – leaned on it for support, and exhaled a breath then placed her hands under her heavy belly to feel the weight of the child and smiled when it moved, jabbing a tiny, careless limb into her ribs.

Feeling content, Ava lifted her arms above her head and stretched then reached behind her and flipped the light switch, allowing brightness to flood the large, beige room. Ava wiggled closer to the sink and examined her plump face in the mirror. She loved the way that her usually pale, dry skin glowed with the beautiful hue of pregnancy. Her dark brown eyes were clear and flecked with gold and she ran a hand over her hair, which hung in long, chestnut waves down the center of her back then fingered the widow's peak whose pointed edge trailed way too far down her forehead. As a teenager, she had been extremely self-conscious about it and had never worn her hair pulled back from her face. Instead, she had worn bangs throughout high school and college. She had also been very self-conscious about the prominent gap between her teeth as well, and had the habit of hiding her smile behind cupped hands.

Ava had never been what others would call pretty, but she was clever, and to Ava, being smart always trumped a pretty face. No, she had no regrets that she was not a beauty queen. One thing that could be counted on was the fading of beauty. Intelligence and quick wit, on the other hand, was priceless.

Her Amir was the best of both worlds. Beautiful and intelligent - masculine and loyal, a great provider and true protector. And she loved him – had loved him since they were young.

They had met in synagogue and were slowly pushed together by their parents. Ava had been sure that a boy as handsome as Amir would never be interested in a girl who was as thick and as plain as she was. And Ava had been quiet and sullen - prepared for rejection.

Amir's reaction to Ava was to avert his gaze and mutter incoherently when he spoke to her, which she found utterly unnerving, but he later confided that he had loved her from the start - that he was tempted by her wide hips and voluptuous thighs; that her ample breasts and small waist were sexy; that she had a beautiful smile.

As Ava mused, the power died and she sighed with frustration. *Amir must have left the coffee pot on again.* How many times had she told him not to use that blasted outlet?

Ava rested her hands on her belly and made her way downstairs to the kitchen to find the pot still plugged into the wall, and she shook her head as she carried the pot to the sink where she rinsed the remaining brown liquid down the drain then threw the coffee maker into the trash.

On her way to the basement door, she thought about snacks and decided on a bowl of peaches and cottage cheese. She descended the stairs slowly, firmly holding on to the banister as she went, being sure that her feet were firmly planted before stepping down. She chortled to herself as she thought of the hissy fit that Amir would have if he knew that she had ventured down the rickety steps alone.

I can't believe you're just traipsing up and down stairs with that stomach, woman, he would chide.

Ava snickered to herself once more as she moved through the semi-darkness and opened the door of the fuse box and began fumbling with switches. When she heard the whirring of the fridge vibrating from the kitchen, she closed the box and headed back to the stairs, her mind once again on peaches. *And graham crackers.*

She noticed the box before she got to the stairs and paused mid-step, wondering where it had come from. True, she had not been in the basement for months, but she was sure that the white, cardboard box had not been there before. The baby moved then, and Ava placed a hand over her stomach and willed the child to be still as she approached the steps, walking around and behind them and then groaned and struggled to nudge the box with a foot, thinking that it was simply an old box of dishes and was surprised to find it to be fairly light, but as the box moved something inside fell over.

Ava groaned and bent at the waist to pull the tape from the cardboard top and then frowned when she folded the flaps back to find a large, leather bound journal inside. Wondering why it had been packed all alone, Ava picked it up then groaned aloud as she stood up, pulling her belly with her.

She turned the journal over in her hands and inspected it. The brown leather was old and worn around the edges and at the spine, but otherwise still in good shape as far as Ava could tell. There was a small padlock holding it closed and Ava fingered the clasp. *Where the hell did this come from?*

She had never seen it anywhere in the house before – had never seen Amir with it. She wondered if her sister, Georgette, had left it behind when she'd visited with them the summer of last year. *I wonder why she hasn't called asking about it.*

Ava turned the journal over in her hands again and mischievous thoughts came to her mind as she thought of popping the lock and reading Georgette's secrets. Ava smiled to herself and tucked the book under her arm then headed up the stairs.

When she got to the kitchen, she went to the utility drawer

and got a hammer and screwdriver then placed the book on the kitchen table and went to work on the lock. She told herself that what she was doing was okay because she and Georgette had always snuck and read one another's diaries when they were girls.

The rusty lock snapped open and Ava laughed gleefully to herself again thinking of the phone call she would make to Georgette later in the evening. No doubt her sister would call her a nosy bitch, but they would laugh and whisper together – confident that the other would keep her sister's secrets as always.

Ava went to the cupboard and searched out a bowl and then fruit and cottage cheese from the fridge before waddling with the book and her bowl back to the bedroom that she shared with Amir.

After sitting the bowl on the nightstand, Ava turned on the bedside lamp and settled comfortably beneath the covers then settled the book atop her belly and opened it. The first words startled her and she quickly closed the journal and laid it beside her on the bed.

Oh, boy. *Don't do it, Ava.*

She exhaled a tempted breath and her eyes strayed again to

the leather bound journal. She lifted her hand and rested her palm on the book, allowing her fingers to trail leisurely along the cover and over the edges of the pages. *Scarlett Ouo Yusef.*

Ava had always liked Amir's mother. She had never spoken much - unlike his father, Tomas, who was always open and direct when he spoke with Ava. She had always felt as if he could see right through her.

Mrs. Yusef, on the other hand, had been a quiet, serene woman – tall and lovely, confident and radiant with kind eyes that were the same whiskey color as Amir's and a luxurious mass of beautiful, waist length black curls. Ava remembered that Scarlett had always worn high heels and pretty dresses; that she was soft spoken and always smelled of roses; that she had been a lady.

Ava had not known her well – not as well as she would have liked anyway. Scarlett had died of brain cancer before she and Amir had married, and Ava remembered that Tomas Yusef's hard exterior had broken - that he had surprised even his son by crying at her funeral. Amir told her later that he had never, ever seen his father shed a tear – not once.

Ten years later, as Ava lay in bed with one hand resting on her stomach and the other caressing the leather of this mysterious book, she wondered if her mother-in-law would mind if she read her private, personal moments to cure her boredom while she carried her son's child. *What would Amir say if he knew?* She had a feeling that Tomas would most definitely mind. Maybe she should call her father-in-law and ask if he knew about the diary – if he wanted it.

Ava again fingered the pages then flipped the book open and bit a fingernail as she quickly scanned the words. She flipped to the last pages of the journal to find that several of them were blank then flipped back to the front of the journal and stared at the first page.

She had already broken the lock, so she was just as guilty as if she had read the journal anyway. Maybe she would read just a few pages and then call Tomas…

CHAPTER TWO

Scarlett,

Keep this journal as my gift to you. Document your adventures, your feelings - your life, so that when you go back later to read them over, you will remember that you are human. I promise that one day you will mend.

Your Friend Always,

Liza Jeffries

March 1960

I'm sitting here near the rose garden with my coffee as always. It is warm to be so early though the sun is not shining very brightly. All is quiet. Amir has begun his lessons and Tomas is – well, I don't ever really know where Tomas is.

But where should I start? Today? Yesterday? From the beginning?

Tomas would say to begin with Ursula since he knows how badly I want to erase that part of my life. Sometimes I think of sending a letter to tell her about the big wolf that I have and how I've thought many times of sending him to relieve Ivan of his wretched existence.

Anyway, as far as the boarding house goes, all was quiet the morning that I departed. Time sure does change a person because now I wonder why I fretted so much about leaving.

I was so afraid. I was so nervous.

I probably would have relented had anyone been around to witness my escape, and had Ursula seen me, I never would have made it to the train station at all. She would have surely awakened Ivan, and the thought of Ivan gave me such fear that I almost passed out as I made my way down the stairs, and though I leaned against the wall for support, I still knocked down a photo in my distress and had to force myself to slow down or I would have rolled down the stairs like a baby ball.

Tears welled in my eyes when I thought of Ivan with his foul smelling breath and his big, clumsy hands grabbing at me, squeezing my buttocks while he tried to stick his retched, foul tongue in my mouth. I had been blessed so far, and someone had always been around to intervene, but I knew that it was only a matter of time before he cornered me with no one around to come to my aid. Even now I can see his sick mind plotting in his dumb head.

Was I so small to myself that I would stay and endure abuse instead of going out into the world to live?

I must admit that I almost succumbed to fear, so afraid was I of the unknown, for this was the only place that I knew how to survive.

It was cool in the house – the fires had gone out long ago – but I burned to memory every worn chair, every phony smiling photo, the heart aching, familiar smell that the room held, and I closed my eyes and swallowed the lump in my throat and hoped that I never saw the place again.

I probably would have lingered there a while longer had a floorboard not creaked overhead and scared the tar out of me. I stepped backwards towards the door, my eyes glued to the staircase, and when my hand touched the doorknob my heart leapt in my chest and my mind imagined Ursula's heavy, hairy feet hitting the floor, and in a panic I yanked the chain from the door, threw it open and sprinted from the house. I could hear a gratifying bang as the door hit the wall though it frightened me

terribly, but I concentrated on the pounding of my feet hitting the
pavement and I took off down the brick walk. I expected that at
any moment Ivan's heavy hand would fall upon me and drag me
back into the house.

By the time I reached Main Street, I had to force myself to
slow down – not because I didn't want to call attention to myself,
but because I was so out of breath that all I could do was pant
like a whipped horse while the cramp in my side throbbed and
threatened to slow me down, but I didn't stop moving – would not
stop. I was finally free from what had been to me a prison for so
very long, and when I saw the train station after such a fearful
walk, I skipped the rest of the way. As I made my way into the
almost deserted station, I twirled in a circle, letting my old dress
fan out about me, and for the first time in the longest time that I
could remember, I smiled...

SCARLETT'S JOURNAL

October 1955

The sun had already begun to rise and Scarlett stumbled

into the train station elated but jittery at the same time. She made her way towards a long row of metal benches then stopped. She was too nervous to sit out in the open and wait for her train for fear that Ursula and Ivan were already out looking for her – would instinctively search for her there in the cool, nearly empty station, so she hid in the restroom and stood by the door, listening intently for her route to be called.

Her mind wandered but she was jolted from a daydream when the door suddenly swung open and an old woman shuffled in on stiff legs. Scarlett had shrieked, fully expecting Ursula's wide forehead and masculine jawline to round the corner, but instead, all she did was succeed in giving the old woman a fright, and the elderly woman screamed before scurrying from the restroom in a huff.

Scarlett exhaled a sigh of relief and pressed a trembling hand to her chest to calm her pounding heart. No more Ursula.

She pulled a white envelope from her satchel and removed several green, wrinkled bills then disposed of the envelope and rolled the bills together and placed them in her brassiere. If Ursula *and Ivan found her, they would most certainly search her bag, and if they found the money she would never have another chance to get away – would have nothing to escape with.*

She panicked as the minutes ticked by with no train. Had it arrived early and she missed it? Was it broken down somewhere? Maybe she had the time wrong?

As she made her way to the platform, she felt as if at any moment one of Ivan's strong, cruel hands would reach out and give her a knock upside the head and she would be drug from the station and raped in Ursula's cold basement. She could almost hear Ivan's gruff voice behind her, and as a reflex, she ducked before turning and searched the faces of the passengers that stood around her.

She was relieved when she heard the loud whistle blowing in the distance, but even after the train arrived, her heart continued to pound hard inside of her chest. As she stood on the platform and handed her ticket to the conductor, she continued to sweat and was so shaken that her knees wobbled as she made her way to her seat. But only then did she finally breathe steadily.

Calm down, Scarlett, she thought. Still no Ivan.

She blinked back tears and hugged her old, blue cloth satchel tightly to her chest while the train jerked and pulled out of the station, and she was reassured by the grinding of wheels on the tracks that she was out of Ivan's reach. No longer would she have to endure Ohio or the old house on Woodbury Lane. No longer would she be called stupid or retarded and met with vitriolic tirades at the end of each tiring day – days when her fingers were raw from scrubbing floors in Ursula's madhouse.

What she would miss was Mrs. Jeffries. Mrs. Jeffries who had taken an interest in her. Mrs Jeffries who had pitied her plight and taught her to read, how to address a letter, how to speak properly. Mrs. Jeffries who put a book in her hands and proved to her convinced, berated mind that she was not stupid.

"No more black eyes, Scarlett."

The old woman had smiled warmly when she handed the envelope to Scarlett. That same aged, caring smile had helped her make it through many miserable days.

She had desperately grasped at those green, rumpled paper

bills and counted them with chaffed fingers while expressing

appreciation through choked sobs. But she had not been ashamed.

"Now you have a chance to be happy, Scarlett. There's not

a lot there, but it's enough to get you started."

As the train wound its way down the tracks and away from

Ohio, insecurity gnawed at her until she wrung her hands and

worried them so that the bleach burns on her fingers began to itch.

What if she starved in a new city?

She looked down at the worn boots on her feet and thought

about the cardboard that she had lain in the bottoms to protect her

feet from the holes that had been worn into the soles. She had her

best two dresses in the satchel and Mrs. Jeffries had shown her

how to fix her hair real pretty. Hopefully, it would not take her

long to find a job.

"You're a beautiful girl, Scarlett. Exude confidence." She

could still hear Ms. Jeffries reassuring voice whispering in her ear.

Yes, she would find a job. No, she would not return to

Woodbury Lane regardless of what happened. She had cleaned in the boarding house for ten years – had carried the load alone since

she was a fourteen year old girl. If worse came to worse, she

would clean houses again in order to feed herself. Returning to

Ursula and Ivan was out of the question. They had almost broken

her body. She refused to let them break her spirit as well.

Eventually, the jostling of the train lulled her exhausted

body to sleep and she dozed in the warmth of the rays of sun that

settled on her through a small window pane and the train slowly

approached Michigan.

When she left the train station in Detroit, she hesitated

there on the concrete, unsure of what to do, and turned about,

letting her eyes roam slowly over the busy street. It was close to

noon and though the sun was out, it was still a chilly day, and

Scarlett envied the women who passed her on the street boldly

donning slacks and men's caps instead of feminine attire.

She walked to the sidewalk and stood still, forcing

pedestrians to side step her where she stood blocking their path.

She stood there like a dummy with her mouth open and watched the brand new automobiles that passed by. The Motor City.

Handsome men in pinstriped suits and slicked back hair sauntered casually along with curvaceous, bobbed hair women hanging from their arms and she stared wide-mouthed in awe at the tall buildings and cars and the dozens of people that thronged the street.

She made her way down the sidewalk through the crowd, stopping from time to time to look into the windows of the many shops that lined the street. The first thing she needed to do was find a place to stay for the night, but her stomach growled and she remembered that she hadn't eaten all day, so she stopped into a nearby diner and sat down for lunch. As she lowered her tired body into a booth, Scarlett exhaled and told herself again that she would be okay.

All that hair. She was beautiful. Anxious, brown eyes and a distressed frown wrinkled her lovely forehead – but the way she smelled - clean. That's what caught his attention – what made him look up from his newspaper when she passed.

Tomas sat back in his seat and pushed his paper to the side and watched the young woman take a booth across from him. When the waitress approached, the woman ordered a cup of coffee then stared down at the menu with a blank gaze. Her hands trembled and she rubbed them together as if agitated, then stopped to inspect them, turning them about before picking at the skin there. She looked up at the door then as if suddenly panicked and Tomas turned, expecting something remarkable, but saw nothing, and a frown creased his own forehead and he gazed back at her with apt curiosity.

Maybe she is a looney, he thought.

His eyebrows rose with surprise when all of a sudden she placed a hand to her small chest, patting and rubbing at her breasts in such a way that would have been obscene had she not carried such an alarmed expression on her exquisite face. He watched as her alarm grew into a frenzy and she began to whisper to herself, and Tomas leaned forward, desperate to hear what she was saying.

What's wrong, kitten, he wondered.

"Breathe."

Tomas sat back again. Breathe, he repeated in a whisper. Ah, she was at the bottom.

"Everything is okay. You're okay." She whispered again.

She turned around in her seat and her head swiveled to and fro as she searched around her then crazily eyed the checkered, linoleum floor. Tomas looked down as well, eyebrows still raised in anticipation as he searched with her and he shook his head then and waited for the look to come – the look that meant tears would soon follow the growing hysteria that mounted in her. And he waited.

There it was...

Tomas shook his head again when she opened her bag and rummaged through it even though they both knew that whatever she sought was no longer there.

Scarlett again nervously ran her hands down the sides of her body and searched the floor beneath the table. It was gone!

Dread fell upon her like a ton of bricks and she pressed her hands to her face to staunch the flow of tears that burned at the back of her eyes. Her head started to pound and she told herself again to breathe steadily. Don't panic...

"What can I get you, hon?"

Scarlett looked up to see the waitress standing over her, pen in hand, poised to take her order.

"I –" Scarlett looked around, wishing that the bills would miraculously appear there on the table in front of her.

"You alright, sweetheart? You look like you done seen a ghost."

Scarlett stared blankly at the woman in her starched, gray waitress' uniform. There was a black net tied around her short, brown hair and stark white teeth shown between thin, red lips – and pink chewing gum that went pop, pop.

Scarlett snatched up her coat and satchel and leapt from the booth all the while looking frantically about her.

Maybe she had dropped it outside...

"You alright, hon?" The waitress asked and placed a concerned hand on Scarlett's trembling shoulder.

Scarlett ran around the woman to the door of the diner with her eyes still wildly searching the restaurant floor.

"You forgot to pay for the coffee, hon. Hey!"

Scarlett could hear the waitress calling out behind her and her voice echoed loudly in her ears. She bumped into people as she made her way back down the street, her eyes now desperately searching the sidewalk.

By the time she looked up, she had lost her way and was so far from the train station that she had no idea where to turn and she became so severely distressed that she leaned against a building and cried – choking because she could not catch her breath, and the few people that passed her on the street turned away in embarrassment.

How had she lost it? Her mind went back to the restroom of the train station and she vividly recalled rolling the bills together and placing them in her brassiere.

Not caring who could see her, she again swiftly glided her hands over her chest before checking her coat pockets. Finding nothing, Scarlett turned and angrily kicked the wall with her *booted foot.*

Why couldn't she do anything right?

Now she had no way to feed herself and the thought of sleeping alone on the street gripped her heart with fear. She looked around desperately, feeling helpless, and did the only thing that she could do – she walked.

She began walking, dazed, unthinking and afraid.

Hot, angry tears streamed down her face as she went and she was so grieved at her loss that she paid no heed to where her feet took her and by the time she looked up, she was alone on the street without another soul in sight.

Scarlett walked – forced herself to put one foot in front of the other while she swiped frustrated tears from her face with a sore, calloused hand. A heavy weight sat upon her shoulders and the urge to give up was strong in her – almost stronger than it had been the day that Ms. Jeffries had handed her those lost bills.

She tried to convince herself that even in her present predicament, she was still in better shape than she had been earlier that morning, and Scarlett squared her shoulders and lifted her head. She would not go back – couldn't.

Without thinking, she turned at the nearest corner - still deep in thought - and mumbled to herself. Surely there had to be somewhere for a homeless, single woman to sleep and she cursed herself again. She was in a strange city all alone and –

Suddenly her air flow was cut off and Scarlett dropped her satchel to the ground and grasped the forearm that dug viciously into her throat. Her heart raced as the odor of breath sour with alcohol and the musty scent of an unwashed man assaulted her nostrils. She was snatched into a strong chest and drug backwards, and as she opened her mouth to scream, a moist hand clasped itself so tightly across her face that it covered her nose.

Scarlett reached behind her and tried to claw at her assailant to no avail and was lifted into the air and pulled off the street and down an alley, and her eyes desperately scanned the street for a passerby as she was drug behind a building. Bile rose in her throat when the hand was removed from her mouth to grope roughly at her breasts, painfully squeezing her nipples until she thought that she would faint with horror. Scarlett screamed as loud as she could and fought harder than she had ever fought Ivan. No!

Her release was sudden and unexpected, and Scarlett fell to the ground then ducked reflexively in preparation of assault. She could never say why she didn't run, but she did not.

She instead stopped and sat staring at the two men in front of her. One was tall and lanky, disheveled and dirty. His cap was pulled down low over his eyes but she could clearly see the snarl on his face as he faced the other man - a man that eyed him coolly, seemingly amused, but with a menacing gleam in his eyes.

He was shorter than his adversary, but stocky and muscular in his brown woolen coat and cap. He rubbed his hands together and blew into them as if warding off a chill, but his head was low as he studied the other man and he rolled a toothpick slowly between his teeth.

"What are you doing?" He asked as if he didn't know.

"What does it look like?" Came the grumbled reply.

And then he moved and grabbed the man by the throat, slamming him to the ground, and her assailant tussled and attempted to fight back, but was powerless against the thick knees *that were applied to his throat and chest.*

Shocked, Scarlett backed against the wall and clasped her hands to her mouth as that knee cut off air supply in an effort to choke the man to death – a man whose cap rolled to the side while his face turned beet red and he weakly swatted and tried to dislodge the leg that choked him into pitiful, sputtering gasps for breath.

"How do you like it?" Tomas asked through clenched teeth, thrilled by the silent plea in the man's eyes.

The sneer scared Scarlett, the wildness in his eyes. He was feral. That's what she realized about him from the start, and though he frightened her, when the gurgling, crunching sounds started, Scarlett hurriedly stepped forward knowing that soon the man's jugular would be crushed, and she threw her hands out in front of her to gain her rescuer's attention.

"You're going to kill him." She said loudly and scanned the alley, hoping that someone would venture by.

It was as if he hadn't heard her – he was so engrossed in damaging the man beneath him. He bit his bottom lip as he leaned more of his weight onto the man and grinned down at him. Cautiously, Scarlett reached out and touched his shoulder then and his arm snaked out, startling her, and grasped her wrists between a hand that was too strong and pulled her to him though his eyes never rested upon her.

"You're going to kill him." She repeated.

"Why are you still here?" He asked, seeming confused, as if what was happening was natural. His voice was rough, like gravel, accented, but clear and authoritative.

"Please don't kill him." She whispered, trying to wrench her wrists free.

He looked up at her in surprise. "He tried to rape you."

"Please." Scarlett pleaded.

To her surprise, he stood, but instead of releasing her, he held onto her wrists even when the man beneath them grabbed his injured throat and tried to climb to his feet but fell over again and curled into the fetal position in pain.

Tomas continued to stare at her, his eyes penetrating, roaming over her with calculated, deliberate interest and she took the opportunity to pull her hands free and took a step back, surprised by his directness. His broad jaw clenched and unclenched as he watched her and his hazel eyes were cold, dangerous. Scarlett felt instantly that there was something wrong with him – something odd.

"Leave." He said to her.

When she didn't budge, he moved toward her and Scarlett instantly backed away.

"Good girl." He said and pointed behind her. "Go that way."

Scarlett stared at him with an incredulous look on her face. "What are you going to do?"

He wanted her to leave badly and though he didn't respond, the violence in his eyes answered her question. Time stood still between them as the disoriented man continued to crawl around on the pavement at their feet and she wanted to tell him to run – scream to him that he was going to be murdered in broad daylight if she left him there.

"What if someone sees you?" She asked quietly.

"Where?" He asked her, the scowl returning to his face as he turned in a dramatic circle and looked around. "There's no one out here. That's why he dragged you back here."

Rage seeped into his face and he turned and kicked the man in the stomach so hard that he dropped to his back again with a pitiful groan.

Impatience set Tomas' hazel eyes ablaze and he again pointed behind her. "Have a nice day, lady."

"I'm not leaving. So go ahead if you're going to do it then." Scarlett said this with more bravery in her voice than she felt.

Though intimidated, her conscious would not let her leave the men alone. This one was definitely stronger than the other, and though she had almost been raped, she knew that something very bad was going to happen if she fled and she didn't want anyone dying because of her.

Tomas wanted to break the man's neck. His fingers twitched restlessly and he balled his fists at his sides in agitation.

How easy it would be to just reach down and grab either side of his head…the satisfying crunch as the dog's bones snapped.

But her eyes would not let him. And he couldn't bring himself to do it in front of her. That's what stopped him and she knew it.

She stepped toward him slowly with her hands out, palms up. "I'm okay. See?"

Her concerned gaze held his own and as the seconds ticked by, he calmed enough that he was able to leave the man lying there on the pavement and he followed her back to the sidewalk.

"I saw him following you blocks ago." He mumbled softly behind her.

She could see that he was ashamed and in spite of everything that had happened, she smiled, surprised that he cared what she thought. He did not raise his eyes to meet her own, and instead, walked ahead of her and picked her satchel up from the ground.

"Thank you for helping me." She said and touched his hand, waiting for him to meet her gaze. "Really."

He studied her quietly before he spoke. "You're very lovely. You should be more careful." He tucked his hands into his pockets and gave her a timid smile. "Come on. I'll get you home."

"No, I'm fine. I—" Scarlett struggled to make an excuse and he watched her with intense, curious eyes. "I'm lost."

"What do you mean lost?"

She confided in him. "I came here this morning from Ohio and I lost everything I had."

"Where are you staying?"

"I don't have anywhere to go." Scarlett squared her shoulders again, trying to shake the weight that had rested there. The fact that she was homeless and had almost been attacked only added to her anxiety.

A poignant look of sympathy came from him then and his hard eyes softened slightly. "I know what it's like to be alone in a new place. Don't worry. I will help you. Okay?"

Scarlett blinked back tears and nodded.

"I am Tomas." He said, placing a hand to his chest.

"Scarlett."

As he led her up the street, she removed a large scarf from her purse and wrapped it about her head and neck to block the wind, and Tomas watched her sullen expression and mused. He had known what she was from the very moment that she had walked into the diner. Just as he had known what was on the mind of the perverted fellow who had so easily fell into step behind her.

Tomas watched her slim back as she walked stiffly ahead of him. She seemed out of her element in this cold, bustling city and he wondered what sort of place she had come from. His eyebrows again rose as he observed her.

Her coat was too big - an ugly, navy blue thing that hung past her knees. Her stockings were the tan, thick kind that old women wore and though he could not see underneath her long dress, he instinctively knew that those paltry stockings were rolled at her knees. But Tomas was more concerned with what was inside those hideous stockings.

She didn't know him, of course, or she would have known better than to go with him, but it was too late - he had already seen her - and her gullible demeanor reminded him of pleasant things –

of memories that he had forgotten, and he wanted to know her.

When they reached the main street, he hailed a taxi.

"Where are we going?" She asked him.

Worry etched her brow and he had an almost uncontrollable urge to massage the frown from her face with his thumbs.

"The Grandmont Hotel. You will be okay there." He noted her hesitation and reached out to grasp her hands in his own. "Trust me."

He left her there at the Grandmont - a large, old-fashioned brick building where a nicely suited gentleman opened the doors and called her "Miss" – where room service arrived pushing a gleaming, silver cart topped with plates of mouth-watering food – delicious buttered rolls, roast beef and gravy, and steamed asparagus.

She removed her shoes at the door then glanced around the room in joyous disbelief. There was a sudden onslaught of rain and Scarlett stared gratefully at the huge raindrops as they beat loudly against the large picture window. There was a great view of the city, and as the sun fell, hundreds of brilliant lights sparkled brightly from below. She turned to the large bed with its gold and beige stitched coverlet and upholstered headboard. She had never slept in anything quite like it.

Tomas had left her there with a promise to return the following day, his eyes telling her boldly that his help went a little beyond that of a good Samaritan. She would be lying if she said that she wasn't attracted to him. Even the rough grate of his voice was appealing.

But there was something off about him and she thought it a bad idea to get involved with him. She closed her eyes and remembered the warm feeling that had washed over her when he spoke to her - the way he hovered above her. The way he overwhelmed her.

She had been very aware of him while they stood together in the hotel lobby – aware of the steady way that he held her gaze and the eagerness with which he tried to draw her to him. It was only a matter of time before he figured out a way to express his interest.

No, she would not depend on his kindness. She would leave the Grandmont as soon as possible.

The following morning, Scarlett left the hotel and went in search of work. She took the newspaper that came complimentary with her breakfast and circled several ads before setting off. After getting lost several times, she finally made her way into the Boston-Edison District and then to a wide, tree lined street that boasted several large, neatly manicured homes and stopped in front of a magnificent three story, Victorian brick house that had a "Housegirl Needed" sign in the window.

Scarlett approached the house and when she walked up the stairs and stepped onto the porch, she read the small words that stood out clearly on a square, copper plate that had been affixed above the doorbell. "The Hospitable House of Viola Little", it read.

Just as she raised a hand to lift the heavy brass knocker, the door swung open and she faced a tall, slender woman who regarded her with curious, lively green eyes.

"Can I help you?" She asked.

"Yes. I'm here about the job." Scarlett responded and silently warned the butterflies in her stomach to cease their churning.

Scarlett stared into alert, wise eyes that regarded her inquisitively. The woman's blonde hair was done in a popular up-do that Scarlett had seen on women outside the train station – the hairdos that she had seen in magazines at the beauty shop where Mrs. Jeffries had her hair colored.

"You a working girl, are you?" The woman asked.

"Yes, ma'am."

The woman regarded Scarlett openly and looked her up and down with a fascinated expression in her eyes – eyes which lingered on Scarlett's worn, old dress and made her cheeks burn.

"What an irresistible quality you have about you." Viola purred. "But why the dark shadows under those big, brown eyes?"

Her question confused Scarlett and she didn't answer. What did it matter?

"Do you have family here?"

"No."

"Did you come here for a job then?"

"Yes." Wasn't that what she had just said?

"Perfect." Viola clasped bejeweled hands together and grinned at her then. "Tell me, how old are you?"

"Twenty-four." Scarlett answered slowly, unnerved at the way that Viola looked her over.

"Where are your parents?" Viola asked intrusively.

Scarlett sighed. "I was an orphan."

"So no one is looking for you then?"

This inquiry took Scarlett aback and she paused and wondered at the peculiarity of the question. Was the woman trying to gauge how desperate she was to have the job?

Viola placed her hands in the pockets of her tailored slacks and leaned against the door. "Do you know where you are?"

"Detroit." Scarlett replied hesitantly, beginning to think the woman daft. She thought again of leaving. This strange woman's prying and questioning about anything other than

whether or not she was qualified for the job was becoming annoying.

Scarlett smiled triumphantly then, suddenly realizing that she had found sense of freedom, and the taste of independence was giving her a feeling of adequacy. She squared her shoulders. Either this woman would give her the job or she wouldn't. Scarlett would refuse to offer her further explanation if she continued with her ridiculous questions, and she pursed her lips and quietly waited as the woman again soaked her up with her eyes.

When that emerald gaze again found her face, Scarlett did not try to hide her impatience, but returned Viola's gaze and did not hide her feelings. To her, the woman was strange.

To Scarlett's dismay, Viola clapped her hands together excitedly and threw her head back and laughed. Her thin shoulders shook with mirth. "Oh, you are going to be a delight."

She stepped to the side and gestured for Scarlett to follow her into the house. The inside was dim and quiet, and the only light came from a back room that sat at the end of a long, carpeted hallway - presumably the kitchen - and a large, brick fireplace that

sat in one corner of the sitting room where an inviting fire burned
and licked at huge logs. An Oriental rug covered the floor beneath
two large, plush brown chaises that sat upon carved wooden legs
in the middle of the large room and gold, velvet shades, which
were tied with braided cord and hung from long bay windows that
allowed sunshine to filter into the opulent space. A black grand
piano sat at one corner of the immaculate room and a handsome,
antique grandfather clock sat against a wall in the front hall.
Scarlett loved it instantly, almost as much as the beautiful, crystal
chandelier that hung over her head from the high ceiling.

"I am Viola." The woman said, extending a bejeweled
hand.

"Scarlett."

She felt uncomfortable as she shook Viola's hand and
again thought of leaving. Maybe she shouldn't work for this nosy,
leering woman...but the house was meticulously clean and gave
her pause. Besides, she needed the money.

She wondered about Viola then. "Is this your home?" She
asked her as she again turned about to view the elegant

surroundings.

"It is, yes."

She heard the flick of a match behind her and turned into a puff of cigarette smoke that escaped from between Viola's burgundy painted lips. Ruby earrings dangled from her pale, delicate ears and she wore black slacks and a white, silk shirt that was unbuttoned to the middle of her small chest. The fragrant aroma of jasmine filled the air around her.

Viola eyes rested on her hair.

Viola had an experienced eye when it came to women. This young woman was way too slim and dark shadows worried her solemn eyes, but she was lovely – dark eyed with lustrous sweeping lashes and a mess of short, black curls that framed a too pretty, heart shaped face. And no doubt a virgin. Viola could smell a hymen a mile away.

She also knew an abused female when she saw one. She would have to tread lightly with this one because the girl was worth a fortune.

"And you're here for what job?" Viola started, choosing

her words carefully.

"The housekeeping job." Scarlett spoke slowly again. Was the woman crazy? "I can cook and clean. When I learn my way around the city, I –"

"Please follow me." Viola interrupted, seeming disappointed.

Scarlett followed her through the handsomely furnished house and up a winding staircase to the second floor where Viola stopped in front of a door at the head of the stairs.

"This room comes with the job." She pushed the door open and gestured for Scarlett to enter. "I can pay you fifty dollars a week." She winked then. "Of course, there's always more where that came from, but that's totally up to you. We all eat meals together in the dining room. You're welcome to join us."

Scarlett stared at Viola with a surprised, raised brow. "You're going to give me the job?"

Viola allowed her eyes to once more leisurely roam Scarlett's body then smiled and took another hit from her cigarette. "I'm sure you'll do just fine."

Scarlett turned and took in the bedroom with its plush, gray carpet and huge four poster bed and nodded to herself. She still thought that Viola was crazy, but she would definitely take the job. Yes, her luck was finally beginning to turn.

Viola winked. "The rest of the girls are out, but they'll be around later."

Scarlett nodded her head to show Viola that she understood. She thought that if she opened her mouth to speak the woman would linger.

When Viola finally left and closed the door behind her, Scarlett stood in the middle of the floor and looked around her in astonishment. A sob caught in her throat and she didn't fight it this time, but gave in to the onslaught of tears. The pressures of the day before seemed to melt away, and as sobs of relief wracked her slim shoulders, she sagged against the wall, feeling as if a building had been lifted from her.

It did not take long to return to the large Victorian house with her belongings. On the way back to Viola's from the

Grandmont, she had thought of Tomas and blushed, knowing that soon he would have the note that she'd left at the lobby thanking him for his help and wishing him well. She had not left him Viola's address for fear that he would come searching for her, and she told herself that she did not need the distraction.

The serious intensity of his hazel eyes when he spoke to her; the strength in the way he held his body, his legs slightly apart as he stood solidly on the cement; but mostly the gentleness with which he treated her...

Of course, she was drawn to him, but she bit her tongue and told herself that it was best to concentrate on getting her life on track. He had rescued her from harm and she would be eternally grateful, but that was where it ended. Scarlett shook her head to clear her brain then pushed him to the back of her mind.

Now back at the large house, she spoke more with Viola about her job duties then climbed the stairs to her room and collapsed onto the bed, sleeping soundly throughout the day, sometimes waking periodically with a jolt, unfamiliar with sleeping in a new place.

As night approached, she opened her eyes fully to the sound of music and voices floating up the stairs to her room – the gleeful shouts and laughter of a party. The noise did not bother her. She was accustomed to sleeping in a house full of people, but she was very curious and left her bed to walk to the bedroom door, and after opening it a few inches, could not help but to step out into the hallway - which she did in her bare feet - and crept slowly across the luxurious, carpeted floor and stood on the top step of the staircase with her hand resting against the banister and listened.

At once, Scarlett was assaulted with a myriad of sounds and smells – cigar smoke, the clinking of glasses, classical music playing from the piano, and most of all, delighted laughter from masculine and feminine voices alike.

Unsure of what to do, but feeling witless for simply standing there, Scarlett slowly descended the steps and stared wide-mouthed at the sight of the many characters in the house. They moved about leisurely drinking brandy from snifters. Men of all types – some handsome and self-assured, others calm and self-

possessed - moved about in tuxedos while beautiful, seductive women threw back their perfectly manicured heads and laughed provocatively. Others sat at the bar or on the laps of men who lounged at card tables chewing cigars and laughing rambunctiously.

Scarlett watched three men in trench coats with their hats pulled low over their eyes enter the house and be helped from their outside garb by a smiling, curvaceous, dark brown woman with long, wavy, black hair.

"Hiya, Mabel." One of the men greeted her by pulling her buxom frame to him and playfully smacking her backside. He was a barrel chested man with a long, white scar that extended from his brow to the corner of his fleshy lips. His thin, black hair was parted on one side and slicked back behind his ears.

Mabel giggled and placed a kiss on his cheek, leaving a red heart-shaped stain under one sleepy left eye. "Hiya, Howie. I been missing you. You ain't been around to see me in a while."

"I know it, doll. I been busy though." He pulled her closer to him and growled while groping her -

"Scarlett, dear."

Scarlett jumped when she heard her name being called and wanted to turn and run back up the stairs to her room. She felt like a child caught in the act. She looked up to see Viola standing at the bar in a red, sequined gown. Her hair was now pulled back into a chignon and she wore a single red rose behind one dainty ear.

She smoked a cigarette from a slim, silver holder, and when their eyes met, she lifted a red, lace clad hand and waved at Scarlett while a tall, gray haired gentleman wrapped an arm about her waist and whispered flirtatiously in her ear. Viola laughed then and winked at Scarlett before turning and giving her companion a frisky swat.

Scarlett smiled shyly down at her own bare feet then turned and took the winding staircase back to her bedroom, sidestepping a couple that approached her on the steps. A tall, long-legged woman descended the staircase in front of her wearing a sheer, black dress and high heeled slippers, and Scarlett blushed, seeing that the red-headed woman wore panties, but no bra.

Her sultry, blue cat eyes settled on Scarlett as she neared her and she smiled, exposing straight, white teeth. "Hi, sugar."

She said in an erotic whisper as she passed.

And Scarlett's eyebrows rose appreciatively at the enticing sultriness of the woman and wondered how she got her hips to sway that seductively. Curiosity got the better of her, and Scarlett turned to watch the pair as they went. Behind her, the woman pulled a short, portly, balding man by his tie, and he trailed her willingly, happily mimicking the provocative, effortless undulation of her hips with a huge grin plastered upon his face as his eyes admired her shapely derriere.

Scarlett went to her room and closed the door behind her then placed her hands on her hips and stood thoughtfully in the middle of the floor.

Viola sure had some interesting friends.

Though the bed felt good, she couldn't lay there all morning. It was still early and she wanted to get the house in order before everyone else began to move around. Feeling content, Scarlett exhaled and threw the blankets back then climbed from the bed still wearing the dress that she had worn the day before.

She left her room and made her way along the hallway to the bathroom, and as she brushed her teeth, she laughed to herself and happily stomped her feet as she thought about Ursula and Ivan surely searching for her even now. But while she dressed, she thought again of Tomas and wondered how he was.

She descended the stairs and moved slowly about the house, noticing with surprise that everything was as it had been when she had first walked through the door the day before. The floors were clean. No glasses littered the tables as they had the night before. In fact, nothing remained of the party but the faint aromas of perfume and cigar smoke, and Scarlett stood confused in her scarf and cleaning dress. Hearing noise from the kitchen, she turned and walked the length of the hallway to the sun-filled room.

"Morning, sugar."

Scarlett jumped then turned to see a short, Spanish girl standing behind her. She was young, like herself, and sported a huge grin and perfectly dimpled cheeks. Her brown hair was shorn attractively in a pixie cut that curled neatly around her small ears and forehead. Scarlett blushed and looked away as the girl sashayed about the kitchen in her bra and a pair of loose corduroy pants. Her small, bare toe nails were painted a vibrant red.

"So you're the new girl. Anna told me that she saw you last night, but I didn't see you at the party." As she spoke to Scarlett her eyes slowly looked her over and Scarlett suddenly felt uncomfortable in her frumpy dress. As if sensing her discomfort, the girl stepped closer and boldly reached out a hand to touch her hair. "Viola said you had beautiful hair."

Not wanting to seem rude, Scarlett simply nodded then stepped away, feeling uneasy with a stranger's hand in her hair. This woman seemed very free and she stared at Scarlett as if she knew her and Scarlett mused again at how interesting Viola's friends were.

"I'm Michael." She said, extending a hand to Scarlett.

A voice rang out suddenly. "Morning, morning."

Mabel floated into the kitchen with a wide, cheerful smile on her pretty, brown face and her long hair now hung in one lone braid down her slim back and came to rest just above her ample

bottom. She went to the stove and started a pot of coffee then

turned slowly and stared at the women with wide, amused eyes.

"I said good morning, ladies."

"Morning, Mabel." Michael said sweetly.

A tall, red-head shuffled into the kitchen then. She stumbled

from side to side and her nightgown was severely wrinkled, but

Scarlett recognized her as the woman from the stairs. She looked

as if she had literally rolled out of bed and she slumped at the

kitchen table and rested her forehead heavily on the polished

wood.

"Coffee." She grumbled from beneath a tangled mess of

hair.

"Morning, Anna." Mabel sung out loudly and she and

Michael chuckled together.

Anna placed her hands to her ears to muffle their piercing

laughter. "My head is pounding." She muttered miserably.

"You know what they say," Mabel started, looking

mischievously at Michael. "The best cure for a hangover is to have a shot of whatever you were drinking the night before. Maybe just a little, hon."

Anna groaned and her head lolled to the side as her cheek searched for the coolness of the tabletop. "If I even smell vodka I'm gonna puke."

Michael snickered again. "Want some bacon?"

"Ohhh." Anna's lifted her head and clutched her stomach.

"How about some fresh air?" Scarlett piped up in a friendly tone.

Anna opened one blue eye and looked over at her.

"I could get you a blanket and we can sit outside until the coffee is ready." Scarlett glanced over to the other women to gauge their reaction. "You should get something in your belly. If you want, I'll make you some toast."

"Who the hell are you?" Anna grumbled which made Mabel and Michael burst into another round of laughter.

"I'm Scarlett, the maid."

They all three laughed then and Scarlett became truly vexed. Her face burned with humiliation.

Anna sat up in her seat and gave Scarlett her full attention. "The maid?" She said in a hoarse voice tinged with a southern accent. "The maid?" She repeated again and looked over at Michael in disbelief. "Excuse me, honey. I'm from Texas, so I'm a little slow, but did she just say that in one week's time, she's gonna think that Viola's real name is something sounds like juggernaut, or did she just say that she was the maid?"

Anna and Michael exchanged a troubled glance and Mabel turned and smiled at Scarlett with a sympathetic look in her almond-shaped, brown eyes. "Sit down, hon. Have some coffee."

Scarlett was furious as she packed her satchel. Ursula was right – she was an idiot. Sounds something like brothel, Anna had said as she sipped black coffee and stared pointedly at her with red, bleary eyes. Scarlett swallowed the lump in her throat. What an ass she was.

Sure, there's a job, Scarlett…I'll pay you fifty dollars a week….Just clean up after the girls, Scarlett.

She mimicked Viola's soft voice out loud as she yanked the blankets up over the bed. What was she going to do now?

Just as she donned her coat, she heard a hard rap on the door and Michael's small head popped in.

"Wanna talk?" She asked in a hushed whisper.

She didn't wait for Scarlett to respond but stepped into the room and closed the door behind her. Over her pants, she now wore a beige, button down shirt with a black belt tied about her small waist. Small diamond hoops dangled from her ears.

"Viola is so mad right now." She said excitedly and pulled Scarlett down to sit on the bed beside her. "She is so pissed at Anna." Michael laughed wickedly, snorting and smacking her knees.

"Why?" Scarlett asked, irritated.

"Because she wanted to tell you herself. She says you're skittish."

"She is a piece of work!" Scarlett exclaimed and Michael laughed even harder.

"Viola said – wait." Michael paused and went still. She held a hand up, her brown eyes darting back and forth as she listened to the sounds coming from outside the door.

Scarlett could hear the quarreling voices of the women as they came up the stairs then there was another hard rap on the door. Michael tried to stifle her laugh behind her hands but tears of hilarity brimmed in her bright, brown eyes and Scarlett scowled at her.

Viola threw the door open then and ran dramatically into the room with Anna close at her heels. Two women that Scarlett had yet to meet stood in the doorway watching the exchange and Scarlett grabbed her satchel, refusing to take part in Viola's spectacle.

"Scarlett, I am so sorry." Viola said, holding her hands out apologetically.

As always, Viola was dressed to the nines. A neatly tailored gray, high waisted skirt and matching jacket graced her lithe frame. Diamond studs sparkled at her ears and on the ring finger of her right hand a large diamond glittered expensively. As the day before, her hair and makeup were perfection.

A slender hand flitted to rest at the base of her throat and her tone was genuine as she spoke, but the expression in her emerald eyes was not heartfelt, and Scarlett cringed at the mock sincerity that easily dripped from her.

"Scarlett, it's not what you think."

"What is it then?" Anna interjected with her hands on her hips.

Viola turned and scrutinized Anna with warning in her eyes. "Shut up, Anna."

"No, Viola." Anna said through clenched teeth. "Tell her where she is."

Viola turned back to Scarlett. "It's true what I said to you. The job is still yours if you want it."

"But if she ever needs a little extra..." Anna said smartly, folding her slim arms over small breasts.

"If you ever want a little extra...well, you're a big girl." Viola shrugged and smiled haughtily. "Otherwise, as I said before, I will pay you fifty dollars a week to clean up after these ungrateful bitches. The job is still yours if you want it."

Viola did not wait for Scarlett to respond but turned and

briskly left the room. Anna stared after her with a look of contempt, but did not speak - as did not the rest of the women - and they parted to let a stiff backed Viola pass through them.

Anna turned to Scarlett and rested her gaze on her. "And what are you gonna do?"

"Leave her alone, Anna." Michael protested now and stood up from the bed with a frown on her face. She turned to Scarlett and smiled. "Let's go for a walk."

"So what are you gonna do?" Michael asked Scarlett as they made their way down the sidewalk.

Scarlett inhaled deeply, enjoying the smell of fall and the sound of dried leaves crunching beneath her feet.

"I don't know." She said softly, worried now. "Seems my luck has been bad all my life." She adjusted the strap of her satchel where it rested on her shoulder and lifted her face to the warmth of the sun filled sky.

"You'll be good at Viola's for at least another two weeks before she throws a tantrum. That'll give you time to find *something." Michael raised her eyebrows questioningly at Scarlett, hoping that she would stay.*

Scarlett shook her head as she pulled her scarf from her satchel. "Nah."

"How'd you come by Viola's anyway?"

"Long story short, I lost everything I had when I got here. I almost got raped, then I was rescued by a gorgeous psychopath, then I ended up at Viola's thinking - like a dumb ass – that I was about to start this grand new life." Scarlett tied her scarf tightly about her head and frowned in utter frustration.

"You almost got raped? Oh, sweetie." Michael pulled Scarlett to her and hugged her.

"It's not the first time." Scarlett replied and pulled away then waved a dismissive hand in the air. "Sometimes Ivan would get ahold of me and dry hump my butt onto a new planet."

"Well – I – okay." Michael nodded, confused, and placed her hands in her pockets. "Scarlett, you can't be out here all by yourself. It's not safe."

"I'll think of something."

"Well, where did you stay the night before?"

"The man I told you about that helped me when that guy grabbed me," Michael nodded as Scarlett spoke, "he got me a room at the Grandmont."

"The Grandmont?" Michael said slowly with a raised brow. "Did he tell you his name?"

"Tomas." Scarlett closed her eyes and tried to recall his last name. "Tomas Yusef."

Michael paused mid-step. "Honey, that man is dangerous."

"I know that." Scarlett snapped with distressed frustration and wondered if Michael had been listening to anything that she'd been saying. "I said he was a psycho. Didn't you hear – " Scarlett stopped and backtracked. "You know him?" Then, "Does he come to Viola's?"

When Michael didn't answer right away, Scarlett shifted her weight from one foot to the other and placed a hand on her hip, impatient for an answer. "Does he come to Viola's?"

"You like him." Michael said calmly.

"I don't have time for that in my life right now." Scarlett

said too quickly and once again adjusted the shoulder strap of the satchel to avoid looking Michael directly in the eye, knowing that she had seemed way too concerned about Tomas' comings and goings.

"No, he doesn't come to Viola's." Michael said, watching Scarlett closely.

Scarlett waited a moment then asked. "How do you know him?"

It was Michael's turn to look away. "I should mind my own business."

They were both quiet for seconds then, both unsure of what to say. Scarlett wanted to coax an explanation from her, but decided against it, not wanting to pressure her.

Michael spoke first, hesitantly almost. "I know where you can find him." She raised her eyes to meet Scarlett's.

They stared at one another for moments without speaking then Michael reached into her pocket and pulled out several twenty dollar bills and stuffed them into Scarlett's hands.

She again pulled Scarlett to her and embraced her. "I can't

have you out here vulnerable and broke. I'll tell you where he is, but you'll have to find your own way."

Tomas saw her standing on the curb in front of the restaurant and his heart started to pound. He placed a hand to his chest. He could not recall his heart ever beating that fast because of a woman and he swallowed as he stared out at her.

Ah, she was lovely.

She had been the only thing on his mind since returning to the Grandmont the day before and finding her gone. He had looked forward to seeing her again – had been looking forward to her - and the thought that he had lost her had been surprisingly depressing. His heart had plummeted as he crumpled the handwritten note in disappointment and the usual dark shadow that had continuously hung over his brow returned to its place.

Tomas calmly removed the napkin from his lap and got up from the table where he had been having a late breakfast and walked outside.

"Scarlett?" He asked, cocking his head to one side. When

she didn't respond he snapped his fingers. "No? Samantha, yes?"

Scarlett smiled widely, knowing that he was teasing her. She came to him and extended a hand which he quickly enclosed in his own. This time she did not look away, but held his gaze directly, letting him know that she didn't want to lose him again.

"I'm glad I found you."

CHAPTER THREE

Ava studied Tomas from over her water glass while he conversed with Amir. Her father-in-law was now past sixty years old, but still rugged and strongly built. He had always had a baleful look about him to Ava - even more so now that Michael had described him to Scarlett as being dangerous.

He hadn't really spoken to her all night, which she probably wouldn't have noticed had she not been reading Scarlett's journal - which she was extremely anxious to get back to - but she knew that she had to be careful. Scarlett had been very important to both Amir and Tomas and she didn't want them to think that she was being disrespectful. Though she had decided to read the book in its entirety...

She had always known that Scarlett was an orphan, but she wanted to know what had happened to Tomas' parents. Ava placed a thumb in her mouth and bit absentmindedly at the nail as she stared at him. Amir had told her that his father never wanted to talk about his parents, and the diary seemed to hold a lot of personal memories that she knew were private, but as her eyes settled on the muscular forearms of her father-in-law, her fingers itched to reach out and trace the faint, crudely tattooed numbers that were visible just beneath the fine hairs that covered them. Yes, she was going to finish reading the journal.

Had it been any other night, she would have tuned Tomas and Amir out as they spoke about the renovations being done to the house, but right now she wanted Tomas to speak to her.

"Tomas, would you like another beer?" She interrupted and they stopped speaking and looked over to her.

"No, Ava. Thank you, dear." Tomas smiled and lifted his glass to show her that beer still remained there, and the corners of his eyes crinkled handsomely as he settled his gaze upon her. As if sensing that she wanted his attention, he leaned forward in his seat and looked her over. "And how are you feeling, Ava?"

She eyed the fine, thin scar that sat in the right hand corner of his mouth and smiled. "Your grandson is a giant."

Tomas knocked twice on the table with a large fist and nodded to a grinning Amir with pride. "Good job, boy."

"Thanks, Pop."

"What will you call him?"

"We're not sure yet." Amir said and got up to clear the table.

Tomas. We're naming him Tomas. Ava didn't speak out loud but stole glances of Amir under hooded lids and wondered why he hesitated in telling his father their child's name. Tomas took note of Amir's sudden change in behavior as well and raised his eyebrows at Ava questioningly and she shrugged her shoulders innocently in response.

"Did you leave room for dessert, Tomas?"

Later that night after dinner was eaten and the game was over, after the dishes had been cleaned and put away, after Tomas went home, and seconds after Amir finally drifted off into a deep sleep, Ava crept quietly from the bedroom that she shared with her husband and made her way silently down the stairs to the kitchen with Scarlett's book tucked discreetly beneath her arm. As she sat at the table and picked up where she'd left off, she was guilt-ridden, and she felt as if Tomas' eyes were burning a hole into the back of her head.

*   *   *

"How did you find me?" Tomas asked as he pulled her chair out and gestured for her to sit in the seat across from his own.

"It's a long story," she responded, unsure of how to explain about Viola.

Tomas smiled, happy that she was there. "Have you eaten?"

"No."

Tomas waved for the waiter and after she had ordered, Scarlett settled back in her seat and rested her hands in her lap. She could feel Tomas' eyes upon her and she didn't speak, enjoying his attention. Tomas sat forward and leaned his elbows on the table.

"I hate that dress." He said and smiled broadly. His thick, dark beard was short and untrimmed and his eyes held a merry glint.

"It'll have to do for now." She whispered, feeling

77

breathless and not at all offended by his dislike of her attire.

"Why are you here, Scarlett?"

"I wanted to see you." She said too quickly.

"I was very disappointed that you left the hotel." He studied her face. "Have you been all right?"

"No." She answered honestly and surprised herself. She did not know why she was so quick to want to confide in him.

"No?" He asked.

"No." Scarlett exhaled. "I'm broke. I don't have anywhere to go."

Tomas sat back in his chair and shook his head with mock sympathy, quietly clucking his tongue. "It sounds like you have a very serious problem."

Scarlett stared down at her hands.

"So you're looking for a job then?"

"I am."

"What can you do?" Tomas leaned forward again and rested his elbows on the table.

"I can cook, clean, mend..." Scarlett started as she

buttered her toast.

"So you're a maid?"

Scarlett paused and looked up at him, wondering if he was making fun of her just as Anna had done earlier, but only saw concern and curiosity in his eyes.

"Yes." She replied, taking a huge bite of the bread.

Tomas lightly slapped his forehead with the palm of one hand as if stunned. "What a coincidence! Would you believe that just this morning I was saying to myself – I said, Tomas, you need a maid."

"Really?" Scarlett replied, enjoying his game. "You're right. That is a coincidence."

"Strange how these things happen, eh?" He shook his head and took a sip from his coffee cup then wiped his mouth with a napkin, and sat back in his chair as if the matter was settled. "When can you start?"

"Well, hold on." Scarlett raised a finger. "Are you difficult to work for?"

"Yes."

"Are you very messy?"

"Extremely." Tomas nodded, but became serious. "You will need to stay in my house of course." He met her gaze directly to be sure that she understood his meaning in spite of their jesting. "You are welcome to any room in the house."

Scarlett nervously fingered her napkin. Common sense dictated that she should not put so much trust in a man that she did not know, and more than anything, Scarlett did not want to place herself in a situation that she would later on regret.

He's very dangerous, Scarlett. She could hear Michael's voice in her head.

"What do you do, Tomas?" Scarlett asked softly.

Tomas sat back in his seat and folded his hands behind his head and studied her lovely face. Her eyes gave away more about what she was thinking than she knew.

Scarlett, Scarlett, Scarlett, he thought, you are mine, mine, mine.

"How did you find me?"

"A friend." She responded without thinking.

"A friend that you have in a new place where you've never been that we both know. Now that is a coincidence."

Scarlett stared down at her hands where they rested in her lap. "Are you dangerous, Tomas?" She asked him directly.

"Yes." He answered her without hesitation. "But do you think that I would hurt you, Scarlett?"

She thought for a moment then answered honestly. "No. I just don't know who you are."

"I don't know who you are. But we can find each other out - together."

When she didn't respond he spoke up again and his tone softened.

"If you are not comfortable with me then I will find a place for you where you will be safe."

They sat for moments without speaking and though she knew that he wanted some reaction from her, she had no idea what to say.

"Do you know what I want from you, Scarlett?" He said this quietly, his eyes smoldering, and leveled his gaze upon her.

Scarlett nodded. Of course, she knew what he wanted. That's why she had come.

"And what do you think?"

"I need time." She answered sincerely.

His gaze settled warmly upon her. "I will take care of you, Scarlett, and you will not run away from me again."

Scarlett nodded and lowered her gaze. His eyes said too much.

"I will give you time. And you will trust me."

Oak Park, Michigan

Scarlett stood on the bottom floor of Tomas' house and wondered what to do. He had brought her here and literally dropped her off, apologizing and telling her that he had business to attend to, but to please make herself at home.

She looked around now and was dismayed at the emptiness of the house. The floors had been polished to an awesome shine, but nothing filled the rooms except for long, dusty drapes in the living room that covered awesome picture windows. Had it not been for the light from the lamp, the house would have been cast into shadows.

The living room was huge. Elaborate drawings had been etched into the oak banister of the staircase, and small lattice window panes graced each upper corner of the large room which sat opposite the dining area and was also bare as well save for the golden light fixtures that hung from the ceiling.

Besides the appliances and cupboards, the kitchen was bare as well. No curtains covered the windows and no towels hung above the sink. Not even a cup remained to be found out in the open. Scarlett opened the refrigerator and let out a soft whistle of surprise at the bare racks that sat inside the frigid box.

Shaking her head, she returned to the stairs and ascended them slowly, admiring the polished, dark mahogany steps that led her to the top floor. There were three doors that she could see – one in front of her and one at either end of the hall, and she walked to the door across from her and pushed it open.

The bathroom was as empty as the rest of the house and, of course, her perusal of the medicine cabinet produced nothing. She

83

left the bathroom and continued down the hall towards the farthest room, and when her hand touched the knob, she paused and pressed an ear to the wood and listened for movement. Hearing nothing, Scarlett pushed the door open and shook her head in disappointment. This room's furnishings were terribly basic except for a large mirror covering the closet door. But she was pleasantly surprised to find a small, stone terrace that led outside and overlooked a lush, green garden that belonged to the house next door.

In the months when the flowers bloomed, the smell that the rosebushes produced was probably delightful, and Scarlett paced the concrete with her arms folded across her chest and closed her eyes as the wind blew through her hair and ruffled the hem of her skirt.

It was quiet out - mid-afternoon - and other than the occasional passerby walking a dog or making their way along the street en route to some destination, all was quiet except for the frequent blaring of car horns in the distance.

Scarlett remembered the room at the opposite end of the

hall and smiled secretly to herself. Tomas.

She left the terrace and made her way out of the room and down the hall then stopped at the door and turned the knob, listening first before pushing the door open.

As the door swung inward, Scarlett's nostrils were thrilled as Tomas' masculine scent hit her full in the face. The drapes were drawn and the room was dark, but she could make out the bed where the sheets lay rumpled from his night of sleep. Without thinking, she stepped inside and closed the door behind her.

She stood there at the door with her heart racing. She knew that this was an invasion of his privacy, but instead of leaving, she walked over to the drapes and pulled them apart, allowing sunshine to flood the dark room. A large bed with a tall, cherry wood headboard sat against one wall and a small television sat on the opposite side of the room. Scarlett smiled as she thought of Tomas staring at the screen with a stoic expression upon his serious face while his steely eyes rested intently upon the actors as they did their best to convince him that the roles they played were real.

Scarlett sighed then closed her eyes and again inhaled his scent as she ran her fingers over a brown leather chair that sat opposite a table where a game of solitaire had been started. She sat down in the chair and hoped that her bottom rested in the exact same spot where Tomas' would sit, and picked up a pair of round spectacles that sat atop the ace of spades and placed them upon her face, wiggling her nose slightly to adjust them across the bridge of her nose.

She mimicked what she thought would be his movements then – his intense eyes studying the cards for his next move, then his strong fingers placing them one atop the other, and she picked up the first card that her hand touched and caressed the edges with the tips of her fingers then brought it to her nose and smiled secretly to herself.

Do you know what I want from you, Scarlett?

She placed the card and eyeglasses back upon the table in the same position as she had found them and got up and walked to the bed and lifted a pillow to her nose, squeezing it tightly as a whiff of Tomas again overwhelmed her senses and the urge to climb into his bed had to be fought by returning the pillow and walking away.

When she got to the closet, she pulled the door open and stared at the neat line of suit jackets and sweaters and pants that hung from wooden hangers. Two lone pair of shoes sat neatly on the floor. There was a box that sat atop the shelf, but Scarlett did not reach for it, thinking that she had gotten too comfortable with his things already.

And though she wanted to look inside his dresser drawers to peek at his socks, she resisted the urge, but did not refrain from taking inventory of the contents which sat neatly on top – coins and folding cash, a shaving kit, a yellowing picture of a young, dark-haired girl wearing a red, checkered scarf tied underneath her chin. The girl did not smile but waved with one hand while she held a small bag of green apples in the other. Her eyes were dark and solemn and the expression on her face was apathetic in spite of her attempt at a friendly wave. As Scarlett placed the picture back where she had found it, she wondered who the girl was and why she was so sad.

Her eyes wandered warily to the item that had first met her gaze when she had approached the dresser – the item that she had tried to overlook. One lone, silver bullet sat in the middle of the polished cherry wood right side up as if purposely placed that way, and she did not touch it but stared at it with enough worry that she subconsciously chewed her bottom lip.

She made her way back to the bedroom door, feeling that she had lingered long enough, but she turned and glanced around the room once more to be sure that she had left everything as she had found it then quietly closed the door behind her.

The streets were still full of people when she made it downtown, and Scarlett felt more confident than she had when she had first arrived in the city. She stepped into a boutique and bought a pair of gloves, a hat that matched her coat, several pairs of underwear, two more pairs of pants and blouses, and smiled shyly to the sales lady as she topped the pile with one pair of red, lace panties.

She made her way to the department store then and

interspersed with the crowd of shoppers. The smell of freshly popped corn filled the air and added to the inviting atmosphere of the warm store and she made her way through the aisles and found what she needed without assistance. She was relieved at how affordable the clothes were and she picked out things that were in style then added a pair of shoes and a new coat, silently sending thanks to Michael for being so kind.

When she left hours later, she found that it was almost dark and she made her way quickly to a cab stand and gave the Oak Park address where she was now living with Tomas.

Living with Tomas.

Scarlett almost skipped up the walk and when she closed the door behind her, she ran to her room and unpacked her purchases before going to the kitchen and struggling to open a bottle of wine, laughing victoriously to herself when she pulled the cork free without making a mess and poured herself a glass. When she had chosen the bottle, she'd had no idea what she was doing and figured that all wine was red and she had been startled to see the clear liquid that filled the glass. She placed the bottle on the counter and smelled the contents before taking a sip. The flavor was sweeter than she had expected and she sipped happily as she climbed the stairs to the bathroom with the bottle in her hands.

As she sunk into a steaming tub of water she felt warmly tipsy, but she grunted as an old, familiar ache returned to her back and she stretched and allowed the heated water to work its magic on her muscles. She sunk beneath the water, submerging her head and shoulders then sat up and smoothed her wet hair back from her face so that tickling rivulets of water ran down her neck and between her shoulder blades and down her back.

After pouring herself another glass of wine, she turned on her side and rested her head on the edge of the tub and closed her heavy eyelids. The warmth of the water combined with the calming effect of the wine relaxed her so much that she lifted one leg until it dangled over the side of the tub, and with her hand propped beneath her chin, Scarlett dozed off into a comfortable sleep.

As she softly snored, Tomas stepped out of the darkness of the hallway and squatted in the doorway of the bathroom with his elbows resting on his knees and watched her. He knew that if he *came any closer he would not be able to help himself from trailing*

his fingertips along the tips of her small toes and then up over a

slim ankle to encircle her shapely calf and thigh only to place a

kiss on the delicate, sensitive skin at the back of her knee.

He stood up then so that he could see completely inside the

large, white tub and rested his eyes on the curve of her bare

shoulder and then on the slender tips of her fingers where they

rested beneath her chin. Her body shifted then and she turned and

Tomas groaned as the brown tip of one moist, succulent nipple

came into view. She was so wet...

Feeling his body harden in response to his thoughts, Tomas

reached above his head and rested his tingling fingers on the wall

to still their restless want to wander, but his icy, brown eyes did

not leave her and settled upon her slightly parted lips purposefully,

knowing that somewhere inside her mouth lay a soft, warm tongue

and this caused a rough, involuntary groan to escape his throat

and he had to force himself to take a step back.

He reluctantly pulled himself away from the doorway and

descended the stairs, exhaling loudly as he disobeyed his body and went quickly to the door. He would not break his promise to her. He would wait for her to come to him, and when she did he was going to partake of her greedily. He meant to taste her starting from the inside out.

The following morning, Scarlett was welcomed by the sun drifting in through the glass of the terrace door. She pulled the covers up to her neck and yawned then stretched and forced herself from the warm, soft bed and out into the cool, quiet hallway. As she walked to the bathroom in her bare feet, she thought she heard someone moving around below and she leaned over the banister to peer down at the bottom floor and found nothing but a still, semi-polished wooden room.

The house was eerily silent as she made her way towards the bathroom and Scarlett wondered if Tomas was home. The floor was cold beneath her feet and she hugged herself tightly and rubbed her hands vigorously over her arms to warm the skin where goosebumps covered her flesh.

After she dressed, she stood in the full length mirror of the closet door and admired herself. The dress she wore was dark blue. The chiffon material was layered and fell just below her knees and Scarlett adjusted a thin belt over her waist then pinned her hair back so that only a few dark tendrils escaped to frame her face. She then added a pair of small, gold hoop earrings that she had purchased the day before and stood back and smiled at her reflection in the mirror, giving herself a curt nod of approval.

Not wanting to disturb Tomas, she made her way to the kitchen in hopes that she would find coffee in the cupboards, which to her surprise were now fully stocked as was the refrigerator and she smiled as she skipped up the stairs to Tomas' room to see what he wanted for breakfast.

She knocked this time before pressing her ear against the door to listen for movement. Hearing nothing, she knocked again and called out his name then pushed the door open and found the room as dark and empty as it had been the day before and Scarlett sighed with disappointment then paused as she stared at the drawn drapes, remembering that she had not closed them when she had left the room the previous day.

Feeling embarrassed, Scarlett's shoulders slumped and she groaned aloud and closed the door. After she had kicked herself with one brand new black ballerina shoe, Scarlett made her way back to the kitchen. She now felt relieved that she had missed him. How dumbfounded she would have been if he'd asked her had she been in his room...

She stood over the kitchen counter and wondered if he was thinking that she had trifled through his things and her face burned with shame. Of course, he knows, Scarlett thought and worriedly bit at the knuckle of her thumb. She was now very, very glad that she had missed him that morning.

After making herself some breakfast and then cleaning her dishes, Scarlett sat in the empty kitchen on the tile floor and rested the back of her head against the wall then stretched her legs out as far as they would go.

Sun from the outside filtered in through the window and as she sat there, Scarlett could hear male voices speaking outside. She rose to her feet and walked to the bare, arched window and stared out at two elderly men standing on the sidewalk engrossed in what seemed to be a hilarious, lively conversation. One gray-haired gentleman held a newspaper under one arm and listened to his companion speak while the other held the leash of a large Doberman in one hand and gestured erratically with the other in a leisurely, joking manner.

Scarlett stood for a while amused by their exchange – by the freedom and genuineness of their boisterous laughter, and then her eyes moved up the street and she watched at least a dozen teenagers pack the corner and wait for their turn to board a large, yellow bus.

Scarlett laughed out loud when a tall girl in a fuzzy, pink sweater swatted at a boy when he ventured too close to whisper in her ear, and Scarlett smiled knowingly at the chatter of the girls in their full, plaid skirts and knee socks, shaking her head at the energetic bounce of their ponytails as they excitedly communicated together. Growing up with Ursula had not allowed time for friends, but Scarlett still understood the value of having a best girlfriend and her mind wandered to Michael.

She did feel safe here at Tomas' house, though he was

never around, but she was terribly bored. Since Michael was the only other person that she liked and knew in the area, she wondered what it would hurt to go back to Detroit for a visit. She remembered how to get there and was sure she could find the large Victorian home. She shrugged her shoulders. And if Viola or Anna made her feel uncomfortable she would simply leave. No big deal.

She decided to wait until later in the afternoon before she ventured out and instead climbed the stairs with a cup of coffee and went back to her room to sit contently on the terrace and watch the early morning movement of the neighborhood, and as the hours passed, Scarlett dozed.

When she awoke later in the afternoon, she felt well rested and stretched her arms way above her head then stood and smoothed her skirt of any wrinkles and made her way to the bathroom to freshen up.

She stopped and stood on the top step and smiled timidly at the bouquet of red roses that lay on the staircase. She held one of the fragrant flowers to her nose and pulled a card from the small, stark white envelope.

+ Dinner at seven? - Tomas

Oh, yes, Tomas, she thought. Absolutely.

***

Tomas took her hand and led her through the kitchen past chefs working vigorously in white caps and aprons, past large brick ovens where fires burned brightly, then past an open mouthed maître d', who in spite of his suave, immaculate, and even controlled appearance, sputtered nervously and greeted Tomas with a bizarre expression on his face.

"Mr. Yusef, would you like me to prepare your table?"

"No, Ulysses. I'll be dining upstairs today. Please send someone up."

Ulysses nodded and stepped aside to let them pass, and as they went, Scarlett could feel his curious eyes upon her, but she didn't look up at him, and instead kept her eyes on Tomas' back as he led her to the upper floor where they could see the entire restaurant from where they were seated.

Jazz music flowed from the stage as a tall, black man in dark glasses blew a catchy tune on a brass horn. His slim fingers

moved expertly over the instrument and when he paused for the
drums, he tapped his feet to the rhythm and drunk from a short,
round glass that sat on a stool beside him.

"You like it here, huh?" Scarlett asked as she settled into
her seat.

"This is my place." Tomas responded and smiled.

"Really?"

"Yes."

After they ordered, Scarlett slowly sipped a glass of wine
and watched the people moving around beneath her. She patted
herself on the back when she didn't grimace at the first taste of the
bitter, red concoction and learned to sip instead of gulp and didn't
frown when her taste buds became overwhelmed. When she took
the third sip, she rolled the wine around on her tongue before
swallowing and relaxed as her brain began to feel warm and calm.

As with every table in the restaurant, their own held a
small, steel lantern and the glow from the light flickered and
played across the table and she lowered her eyes to his hands and
watched the shadows play across the fine, dark hair that covered

his strong fingers. He was dressed neatly in a sweater and dark slacks, and Scarlett smiled again at the surprisingly neat bushiness of his short beard and mustache then lifted her eyes and returned his smile.

Tomas was not handsome, but he was ruggedly male, rough around the edges and extremely masculine, and Scarlett trembled inwardly at the heat of his intense gaze as he fixed his eyes upon her.

"Are you comfortable at the house?" He asked, leaning forward and running his eyes gently over her face.

"I am, yes."

Scarlett remembered his bedroom drapes and her face burned but she did not avoid his gaze, and silently prayed that he had forgotten or simply wouldn't ask her what she had been doing in his bedroom.

Tomas scratched the side of his nose with a thumb while he studied her face. "Is there anything you need?"

"No, I'm fine." She said a little too fast. "How are you?"

"I am better now that I am with you. You are so lovely,

Scarlett."

"Thank you, Tomas." She responded softly.

Tomas leaned forward and held her gaze and as he stared deeply into her eyes he whispered, "You are very lovely."

Scarlett found solace in the fact that he could not see that the butterflies that floated and flipped about inside of her belly had started to melt and ran in a pool down her calves and into her shoes where her toes had already begun to curl beneath the table.

He sat back in his chair and folded his hands behind his head and looked at her with such gentleness that the butterflies turned to jelly. He hardly blinked as he watched her and she saw in his eyes what he was thinking – could feel his longing, in fact, and she sighed with pleasure and the room went still then, and for Scarlett the music stopped and no one remained but she and Tomas. She wanted to climb into his lap and place her ear to his sturdy chest and search for the sound of his heartbeat.

He reached across the table and enfolded her hands in his own and Scarlett's eyelids closed briefly, blissfully, as he made a lazy circle in the palm of her hand with the calloused pad of his *thumb. He paused mid-stroke and searched each of her fingers then and Scarlett knew that he was staring at the roughness of her hands, but she didn't pull away, and instead allowed herself to enjoy the feel of him exploring her, then he bent and touched her with his mouth, and she froze as he placed a warm, lingering kiss in the palm of each of her hands and Scarlett could've sworn that her legs melted into her shoes as well. When his warm breath fanned across her palms, a delicious chill ran down her spine and she could not help herself from reaching out and touching him. She let her fingers sink into the coarse hairs of his beard then shivered as he placed a soft kiss on the tender tips of each of her fingers.*

They were both disappointed by the waiter's interruption, but they settled into easy conversation as they ate, and Tomas enjoyed an unusually light mood as he dined with Scarlett. She was very considerate of him and extremely attentive and he relaxed and conversed with her with a peaceful ease that he hadn't felt with anyone for longer than he cared to dig into his memory to recall. She watched his mouth as he spoke and this delighted him tremendously and as her eyes caressed his lips, he knew that his torment would soon end.

He could hardly wait to hold her in his arms and bury his face in the mass of soft curls that covered her head. His eyes took in the thickness of her eyebrows, the comical facial expressions she made when amused, the pretty pertness of her nose and the way the tip tilted upwards and begged to be kissed and then his gaze settled on the sensual curve of her bottom lip and remained there.

He nodded sometimes in response to her questions and at other times engaged with her in an exchange of words, but he mostly wanted to listen while her soft voice tantalized his ears and he indulged himself in the sweet tranquility that her company provided.

They stayed out late and by the time they returned, Scarlett was giddy and light headed, and with Tomas' assistance, she made it out of her coat and up the stairs to her room. She had not fallen asleep right away, but had lain awake listening to Tomas move about in his own bedroom and then in the bathroom. She must have dozed off momentarily because she snapped awake with a jolt as the downstairs door closed with a loud thud and she knew by

the deep silence that could be felt as well as heard that Tomas was

gone again and she forcefully exhaled an indignant, exasperated

breath.

She pulled her robe tightly about her now and mumbled

grumpily to herself as the loud chattering of children floated to her

through the kitchen window.

She refused to sit alone today and after donning a pair of

blue jean peddle pushers and a blue, plaid blouse, Scarlett tamed

her unruly hair into two French braids then grabbed her coat and

left the cold, empty house. Her mood instantly lightened as she

stepped out into the coolness of late morning. She smiled to herself

and decided that she would find a way to enjoy her time until

Tomas returned.

After the ride to Viola's house, Scarlett felt content and

upbeat, and when the bus let her off at the corner, she quickly

walked the two long blocks to the house with her head down and

her hands in her pockets. When she stepped onto the porch, she hesitated before knocking and pulled at the fabric of her gloves nervously before lifting the heavy knocker and waiting.

The door swung open and Viola stood in front of her with a sly grin on her face and appraised her slowly - much the same as she had done when they had first met. Viola's straight, blunt cut hair bounced softly around her shoulders, and as always, her makeup was flawless. She wore a string of pearls around her neck and several strands around her wrists. A peach, silk pants suit clung attractively to her slender form.

"Well, come in, Scarlett." Viola chided her as if she weren't the one being ridiculous. "Don't just stand there gawking at me."

Scarlett stepped into the house and closed the door behind her then followed Viola inside, walking in the trail of her expensive, jasmine perfume. They went into the sitting room and Viola sat down upon one plush chaise and bent over a small tray, lifted a rolled dollar bill to one nostril and sniffed a thin line of white powder up her nose then innocently held the tray out to Scarlett as she wiped some of the substance up with a finger and *rubbed around inside of her mouth.*

Scarlett shook her head in disbelief and Viola rolled her eyes and sighed as she sat the tray down beside her. She then rubbed her nose between perfectly manicured fingers and sat back and lit a cigarette. With glazed eyes, she lazily looked Scarlett over through a puff of white, swirling smoke.

"Sit down, Scarlett." Viola said softly and lightly patted the cushion next to her.

Scarlett removed her coat and sat down in a soft, high backed chair on the opposite end of the room.

Viola smiled naughtily at her and leaned forward. "Are you still upset with me, dear?"

"No, Viola. I just don't trust you."

"Trust me?" Viola said as if Scarlett were being absurd and sat back in her seat again, puffing at her cigarette. "You were in a very precarious position, darling, and I simply tried to help you."

Scarlett smacked her lips sarcastically.

Viola placed her lips to the long, black cigarette holder

that she held between slender fingers and watched Scarlett through cunning, greenish gold flecked eyes and long, lowered lashes. "And how have you been making out, dear?"

Scarlett could read Viola's mind and she shook her head at the shrewd, rapacious nature of the woman, thinking that Viola would sell a boil off of her own mother's backside to turn a profit.

"I'm actually doing pretty good, Viola. Thanks for asking." Scarlett told her but stared at the woman with wary eyes.

"I'm glad to hear it. But if you ever need a job..." Viola allowed her words to trail off and stared at Scarlett with a wicked, playful look in her eyes.

"Is Michael around?"

"She is." Viola let the words hang in the air.

Scarlett waited and met the challenge in Viola's eyes.

"We're having a party tonight, Scarlett. Would you like to join us?"

Party? Scarlett hated to admit that she was curious, and she knew that Viola knew it as well by the satisfied grin that she gave her.

"Nothing would happen that you don't want, dear." Viola puffed on her cigarette as she observed her. "And, of course, Michael will be there."

Scarlett smiled wryly at Viola. "I'll think about it."

Viola nodded and walked over to the bar, "Drink?"

"No." Scarlett stood from her seat. "Michael?"

"Upstairs."

Viola gave her a full view of her back then and Scarlett, feeling dismissed, turned and climbed the carpeted staircase to Michael's room and knocked.

"Who's there?" Michael said from the other side of the door.

"It's Scarlett."

The door swung open and the young woman pulled her into a bear hug, squeezing so hard that she almost choked Scarlett with her slender arms.

"I was so worried about you." She said excitedly and pulled Scarlett further into the room. "Did you find a place to stay?" Michael's bright eyes bounced over her and she knew that

Scarlett had something to tell.

Scarlett smiled and shook her head, unsure of what to say. In one week she had escaped Ursula, caught a train to a strange place, became penniless, almost had her feminine wares sold right up from under her, and moved into a house that belonged to a man that didn't live in his house. She shook her head again and pursed her lips, resigning herself to the craziness that was her life.

"What is wrong with you?" Michael asked curiously.

"Nothing." Scarlett said this with a nonchalant shrug. "Nothing."

"Where have you been?"

Knowing how Michael felt about Tomas, Scarlett hesitated before she spoke. "With Tomas."

"Are you crazy?" Michael exclaimed and grabbed Scarlett by the shoulders.

"What is the problem, Michael?" Scarlett got up from the bed, irritated by Michael's behavior.

Michael leapt from the bed and hurried from the room while Scarlett paced the carpet in an almost agitated state.

Michael then came back a moment later pulling a grumpy, sleepy eyed Anna behind her. When Anna saw Scarlett standing there she pulled away from Michael, slid her sleep mask slightly down over her eyes and clumsily straightened her nightgown and tried to shuffle out of the room.

"Tomas." Michael called this out in a sing-song voice and Anna stopped dead in her tracks and turned.

She pulled the mask over her forehead and smiled charmingly at them. "What about Tomas?" She asked sweetly, reaching out and grabbing Michael's hand.

Michael looked over to Scarlett to be sure that she was watching then steadily held Anna's eyes, and Anna turned as if struck by lightning and fixed her eyes on Scarlett. Her blue gaze was steady, and without speaking, both women understood, and they both stood stock still – Anna with a challenge in her eyes and Scarlett feeling secure because they both knew intuitively that Scarlett had the upper hand, and she smiled inwardly knowing that Anna wanted Tomas and that he clearly didn't want her or she would be the one in his house. Scarlett shrugged at Anna then smiled.

Though her eyes glittered with jealousy, Anna smiled prettily, confidently. "You have no idea what to do with him."

"To hell with that," Michael pointed to Scarlett but addressed Anna. "Tell her he's dangerous."

"I just told her she can't handle him. I'm tired of warning her, Micha." Anna smirked and shook her head as she sauntered from the room. "Be careful, little girl."

Finally, he was home. She had tiptoed from her room and across the dark hallway to his bedroom. She could hear the steady rhythm of his breathing through the door, and thinking him asleep, Scarlett quietly laid her hand on the knob and turned it slowly, pushing the door open just an inch and gasped softly at the sight before her.

As always the warm, masculine scent of him assaulted her senses, and against her will, her eyes fluttered closed and a soft sigh escaped her lips. He lay on his back in the midst of the huge bed with just a sheet draped across his lower body. A pillow rested slightly across his face and his chest rose and fell steadily as he slumbered. Her eyes rested on his hands before trailing up over his tanned, muscular arms and then to his broad chest which was sparsely covered with fine, dark hair. She frowned for a moment, wondering about the deep, jagged scars embedded in his arms and torso...

His abdomen, taut with finely corded muscle, was also covered with dark hairs and a line of soft fur extended from above his navel and ended under the lone, navy blue sheet that hid the rest of his body from her view - everything except two of what she thought were the most beautiful feet that she had ever seen.

She slowly looked him over once more before lifting her gaze then gasped with embarrassed surprise when she found him watching her. His dark eyes peered at her from beneath the pillow – his gaze was direct, searing her flesh and she suddenly felt flushed and hot all over. His outstretched arm turned until his palm lay face up on the sheet and he beckoned to her with his fingers.

Scarlett felt as if her feet were glued to the floor. She raised *her eyes again and he pushed the pillow away and watched her,*

placing his hands behind his head and lifting his upper body to see

her more fully yet still she could not move. When his feet hit the

ground, and he got up from the bed and moved toward her, she

became light-headed and her mouth went dry. He moved

purposefully, tempting in the way he stalked her, his pupils dark

and wanting, him naked and virile and her loins began to melt. She

pressed her thighs together but continued to feast her eyes upon

him.

He was so close…

When he lifted her off of her feet and carried her to the bed,

Scarlett moaned in weak protest as the large strength of his body

engulfed her in delicious, pulsating heat.

"Tomas, wait…"

A gentle whisper as her nightgown slipped over her head to

be tossed carelessly to the floor and then a soft, sensuous, "Shhh."

CHAPTER FOUR

"...man is stronger than iron. *C'est la vie, mon cher ami* – to pass, to last, to cast aside." Ya'akov Gabbai, ***We Wept Without Tears***

February 1940

Kazimierz, Poland

"They bombed Warsaw all to hell. People were delirious, half-crazed, running mad in the streets while buildings collapsed all around them."

Jakob Alter whispered harshly to his sister and brother-in-law where they stood together in the empty kitchen of his home. He was a wiry, middle-aged man of average height with thick, wavy gray hair and a deep Yiddish accent. His bespeckled eyes squinted and he pulled roughly on a long, graying beard.

"All of those people killed by the bombs. The women are saying that they were pulling babies from beneath the rubble by their little feet." Miriam whispered to the two men.

Avigail turned and stared at Tomas with a shocked, wide-eyed expression on her face. She and her brother stood near the kitchen door and eavesdropped on the conversation between Jakob

and their parents who stood in the kitchen speaking in hushed

tones.

The home was dark, but the light from a lone tallow candle

in the sitting room cast dark, flickering shadows along the wall.

Tomas impatiently placed a finger to his lips to signal to his sister

to be quiet and tried to concentrate on what he was hearing. Had it

not been for Avigail, he would have stepped into the kitchen and

questioned his uncle - respectfully, of course - but Avigail thought

it improper for them to join the conversation and persistently

persuaded him to remain outside with her, but as soon as they

realized that Jakob was speaking of the camps, they had stopped

their whispered bickering and listened intently to everything being

said, knowing that there may be news from outside.

Tomas knew in his bones that something bad was going to

happen. It bothered him so much that he could hardly sleep at

night. The SS looting of homes was constant. They boldly intruded,

making themselves welcome in homes where even the art was

snatched from the walls while blood ran from the mouths of mothers who begged for mercy whilst clinging to crying infants.

"Yes, yes. The air strikes did miserable harm. With that heavy of a bombardment, it was only a matter of time before the Poles were defeated." Jakob responded quietly.

They had come upon him by surprise – had nearly scared the life out of him when they entered unexpectedly to find him hiding a handkerchief filled with cash and coins in the wall.

He had nervously tried to explain with a wave of his hand, "They have started to take our property and I don't want to lose everything that I've worked so hard for so..."

"Why not hide it? They are stealing from us." Gideon told his brother-in-law bitterly and without judgment. "Coming into our homes and searching through our things to take whatever they want for themselves and then damaging the rest."

"If we cooperate then this will all go away, Gideon. We can start over." Miriam said.

Gideon sighed and ran a large, calloused hand through his dark hair. For a while now, he had begun to think that his wife was becoming soft in the head.

"You're living in a dream world, Miriam. They've taken our radios, they work us and our children like mules, they beat and shoot people in the street without provocation. And what about the others? Sent away never to return, that's what. Wake up, wife, and look around at what's happening."

Jakob nodded in agreement. "I can understand them stealing from us, Gideon. But greed is no excuse for their inhumanity, I tell you. And the way they behave like murderous fiends. They are depraved, diabolical –"

"Do you remember, Miriam, the German camps that I told you about where they work the people to death – kill them with exhaustion and hunger?" Gideon addressed his wife in a whisper.

"You two are not the only ones who hear things. Those places are for political prisoners and homosexuals." Miriam said in a voice that was a little too high pitched. She still refused to believe what was happening.

"Those camps are for Jews too, like me and you, and Jakob – like our children." He whispered louder this time and fought the urge to grab Miriam and shake her. "You saw with your very own

116

eyes what they did here – "

"It's because of the Polish, Gideon. They have brought this curse upon us. They only hurt the Jews because we are God's people. God will -"

"Yes, yes. The Polish are suffering as well." Gideon interrupted, as if he were trying to beat the words into her traumatized mind. "But there is no partiality with God, Miriam."

"Look at what they are doing here – even in Warsaw. Do you know what that is saying? I tell you they think even less of us than they do of dogs." Jakob exclaimed suddenly, pointing a finger into the air and vehemently smacking the band that he wore around his upper arm. "We are to be registered for a reason. And I will tell you another thing - no one will come to our aid."

"But the Council says – " Miriam started, but was interrupted by Gideon holding up an impatient hand to signal for her silence.

His voice was strained as he spoke. "As far as I am concerned," he said, "the Council is only good enough to round people up to work in the harsh, freezing cold most times in hunger, to supply the German labor quota. That is all, Miriam."

Tomas looked over to Avigail to gauge her reaction to the conversation going on in the kitchen. Her head was bowed, but he could see the confusion in her face as she traced the blue star that was sown onto her armband with the tip of her index finger.

Avigail had not wanted to wear the band – had cried even. She knew that it was meant to set her apart, to belittle her into thinking that she was worth less than another human being – someone who had somehow been deemed more valuable than herself by some ignorant, tyrannical power, though every human that she had ever encountered had only one head and two legs, just as she did, and she was certain that their blood ran as red as her own.

She hated to hear the Nazi officer's conversations when they spoke to one another in the streets. She understood well what they were saying and knew that their evil hearts were void of God.

Tomas knew what really hurt his sister – being denied the right to openly practice her faith, and almost as equally, being denied her education. He saw the shame in her face when they first *had to wear the star in the streets.*

Avigail had been raised by their mother's sister, Ruby. Aunt Ruby had been barren, and since she and Miriam had always been so close, when Avigail reached school age, Miriam and Gideon had sent her to live with Ruby and her husband Georges in Berlin with Avigail returning home to Kazimierz during breaks.

When she became of age, Avigail returned home permanently and married Rye, a pious young man whom she had loved since she was a small girl. Now seven years later and poor Avigail was a widow, Rye having fallen ill and expiring from dysentery. But she had remained optimistic, and her hope had been to become a teacher, and the fact that she was now forced to put her education on hold until after this chaos ended pained her a great deal.

Tomas was not as sensitive as his sister and had known exactly what the armbands meant, and he agreed with his uncle and father wholeheartedly. Something very bad was happening – something that went beyond the happenings of regular warfare.

Tomas stared at Avigail's bent head and clenched his fists and wished that he was stronger. They were being treated like animals and were powerless to fight back. At eighteen years old, Tomas had his own ideas, and as his father told him and he agreed, he was no longer a boy.

He was as tall as Gideon already, dark-haired and husky like his father as well, but with a dark frown that always shadowed his young face. Tomas had always been a serious, brooding young man with a strong character...though he was prone to trouble, which distressed his parents greatly. His father lectured him often about his roguish behavior and the importance of mending his ways.

Gideon had wanted him to become a doctor like his grandfather, but that dream seemed almost impossible to Tomas now. He scowled, deep in thought, and frowned at the scarf on his sister's head. Avigail noticed Tomas watching her and stuck a tongue out at him and he grinned.

He hated to leave Avigail alone these days, especially in the newly ruled streets of nearby Crakow, and some nights he would jolt awake to a heavy feeling of dreadful foreboding having *had visions of her being torn apart by snarling, hungry dogs.*

She was tall and strong, resilient and raven-haired, athletically built like his mother, but she was no match for the constant danger that loomed over them, and he chastised her constantly about the importance of staying by his side. His sister had been his very first ally. He loved her very much and he would die before he watched her be soiled by vicious hands.

"Now is the time to go."

Jakob whispered this so low that Tomas barely heard him and he was tempted to go to the kitchen and sit with them to help draw up a plan, but Avigail elbowed him into the wall.

"Go where, Jakob? We should have left at first when everyone else fled. They are everywhere now. Where will we go? How will we go?"

"I don't know. Anywhere but here, Gideon, because mark my words, things are going to get much, much worse..."

July 1940

She had been standing in the window while the others

hurriedly packed whatever small possessions they could carry. She

would not walk behind the winding, weeping snake – she did not

want to become a part of it. She'd heard Gideon rush into the room

with Avigail, and the noise he made as he hurriedly threw their

possessions together banged loudly in her ears and she could have

sworn her brain was sliding off of its shelf. Gideon's deep voice

sounded far, far away as he directed Avigail to take her mother

and pack a small bag.

"Hurry, Miriam. There's not much time." He told her.

"It's past curfew, Gideon. We cannot go." She pleaded.

Miriam wept into her handkerchief and tried to think of a

way to make her husband see reason. She couldn't believe that this

was happening and every day that her mind drifted away from her,

she found it harder and harder to stay in touch with what was

going on with her family.

"It's only late morning, Mother, and we have to go."

Avigail said gently to Miriam though she felt the cold hand of

panic squeeze her own young heart. "Don't you hear them yelling

in the streets?"

Miriam looked over to her daughter then turned slowly about the room, frantically searching for the loud tones, and her eyebrows rose and she stood with outstretched hands and soothingly made a plea to the wall as if attempting to calm its wrath, and Avigail pulled her mother to her and hugged her tightly before pulling the shawl from Miriam's shoulders and securing it around her head and neck.

"Mother." Avigail said to her again, giving her a little shake in the process. "The SS are going to be coming up soon. We have to go."

"I will make them coffee, Avi." She placed a trembling hand to Avigail's cheek to reassure her daughter that everything would be all right.

Her innocent Avigail, nearly thirty and childless - already a widow.

Gideon rushed back into the room then and almost tripped over a bag as he moved quickly towards her.

"It's only a matter of time, Miriam. We must go now." Sweat covered his brow as he grabbed her by the shoulders and steered her shocked body towards the door. *"Wait here. I will wake Tomas."*

"He is sick. I will wake him." Miriam said.

As he attempted to push her unwilling body towards the door, Miriam escaped Gideon's grasp then stopped suddenly, silently, as the menacing frames of two SS men filled the doorway.

"Why are you still here?" An SS officer stood with his hands behind his back observing them while another larger, fiercer looking man stood behind him holding a long rifle. Hate dripped from the officer's toxic tone like sharp knives and Avigail cringed and hid behind her father.

"Our son is ill. I am going to wake him now."

"Stop!" He replied, suspiciously eyeing Gideon from his head to his feet then back up again. He walked directly up to Gideon, who lowered his eyes, and whispered in his face. "We cannot even expect you people to follow simple instructions."

He searched Gideon's downturned face for any slight sign of insubordination, and Avigail, though she did not raise her eyes either, prayed that her father was not ashamed and her heart seethed with anger for the unfairness of their situation. Her pride in her father was not lessened because she knew that if they stood on equal ground Gideon would have thoroughly checked the man.

"Search the house, Heinrich." The SS man said over his shoulder to the uniformed giant behind him. He kept his eyes steadily upon Gideon's lowered head.

Avigail sent thanks to heaven that though the stone-faced man attempted to provoke Gideon to anger, her father held his composure. Avigail knew that it must be demeaning for him to have the light-haired man speak to him so closely in his face that Gideon could surely feel his hot breath touch his mouth, his nose - and Avigail exhaled a pent up sigh of relief as the vindictive officer was distracted by this Heinrich, who was grunting about a sweaty Jew lying asleep on the floor.

"Don't move. One step." The SS man said, eyeing them all harshly before turning sharply on his heel and walking away.

Miriam waited until he was out of earshot then whispered feverishly to Gideon. "There will be Germans no matter whether we're here or anywhere else."

"Shh." Gideon shushed her and strained his ears to hear what was going on in the next room.

Miriam grasped her husband's hands tightly in her own and they watched in angst as the men disappeared into Tomas' bedroom.

"The children's lives are in the hands of Germans no matter where we are, Gideon." Miriam continued to babble. "Please don't let them send us away."

They waited there in the suddenly cold room as Tomas was awoken from a sick sleep and Avigail cried out when she heard her brother's confusion met with brutality. Hot, frustrated tears burned a trail down her cheeks and pooled beneath her chin...then a sigh of relief as her mother held Tomas to her. She watched her father's jaw clench and unclench as a myriad of emotions played across his face at the sight of Tomas' bloody face and ill stricken eyes.

In the end, they crowded together on the street with the rest of their Jewish neighbors. Tomas could –

***

"What are you doing, Ava?"

As a reflex, Ava slammed the journal shut at the sound of Amir's voice behind her and regretted that she could not stop time long enough to hide the journal on a shelf in the refrigerator then put Amir back to bed, but he was standing over her already, and when she looked up at him, sheepish and shame-faced, she could tell by his countenance that he had been standing there for some time and knew exactly what she was doing. Her first instinct was not to lie but to placate.

"Let me explain, Amir."

Amir grabbed the book from her hands and opened it, then after scanning a few pages stared at her, mouth agape with his eyebrows raised in surprise. "Why didn't you tell me?"

"Because I knew I shouldn't be reading it." Ava admitted with her hands clasped tightly together in front of her as if praying.

"Where did you find it?"

"In a box in the basement. You didn't know about it?"

Amir shook his head and frowned down at her and Ava apologetically returned his stare. *Let's read it together*, she desperately wanted to say and he knew it, and Ava was again ashamed.

"Forgive me, Amir."

Ava leaned upon the table and lifted her heavy body from the chair. She walked over to Amir and smiled again, placing her hands against his chest and looking into his eyes.

"Forgive me?"

Amir didn't speak but turned away from Ava and left the kitchen with his mother's journal grasped tightly in his hands. Before Ava even heard the bedroom door locking, she was making her way to the linen closet to get sheets for the guest bedroom.

The next morning was a Saturday, and Ava was glad because Amir would not work on the Sabbath and she would have all day to find a way to smuggle the book from him. She had risen early that morning and sat in the cool kitchen guiltily thinking of a way to convince Amir to let her finish reading the diary. She had hardly slept the night before so heavy on her mind had been the journal.

Now at a quarter to twelve in the afternoon, Ava sat on the

couch in her nightgown biting her nails and listening for any sign that Amir was stirring upstairs. *If he left the house would he hide the book from her or take it with him?* If he left without it, there was no way that she would be able to sit still and not search for it. *What if he told Tomas?* The thought made her cringe. *He wouldn't tell, would he?* No, he loved her. Besides, Tomas was old-fashioned and would blame Amir for not being the man of his house and Amir could never handle his father chastising him.

Ava pushed herself up from the couch and slowly took the stairs to their bedroom. When she reached for the knob and twisted it, she was surprised to find it unlocked and she quickly stepped inside. The shades were drawn and only the small bedside light illuminated the room where Amir sat atop the patchwork quilt in a sweater and long johns with a pair of reading glasses perched atop his nose totally engrossed in the worn, leather journal.

"Amir!" Ava exclaimed with her hands on her hips.

Amir jumped and looked over his shoulder at her then back down at the diary.

"How far did you get?" He asked after several seconds.

Ava nearly skipped over to the bed and plopped down beside him. He turned and looked at her with a smirk on his face and Ava had to stop herself from shrugging her shoulders.

"I'm supposed to be on bed rest, Amir. How can you be so cruel? I'm carrying your child and you throw me out of our bedroom." Ava said this sweetly to her husband with lowered eyes.

"You are so full of it." He stated this matter-of-factly and they laughed together, knowing that he was right.

He leaned over and placed a warm kiss on the tip of her nose then one on her chin. "I don't like when you keep secrets from me, Ava."

"I know, sweetheart. I was desperate."

She could tell that his interest in the book had also been piqued, and unwilling to let this opportunity pass her by, she clasped her hands to her chest then looked down at the journal and back up to Amir with a plea in her eyes.

"My father can never know that we read it." He held the book up and said this in an urgent tone and his deep brown eyes displayed the utmost seriousness.

Conspiratorially and without speaking, Ava looked him solemnly in the eye then crossed her heart with an index finger and raised her right hand high into the air. "Okay."

He stood and pulled back the covers for her to climb beneath them and she slid in next to him. While he placed his glasses back atop his nose, Ava leaned her head on his shoulder and cuddled up next to him and closed her eyes as his deep voice took her back in time.

CHAPTER FIVE

January 1941   *Warsaw District*

Tomas sat quietly by himself in the corner of a cold, vacant, rubbish filled room in an abandoned store on Mila St. and smoked a cigarette from a pack of tobacco that he had stolen off of an inebriated Polish officer who had been too distracted by a pretty ally, Ania, who had been showing him the curve of her shapely thighs. While his fellow officers stood outside and harassed a dementia stricken old woman who begged passerby for food, two young men pilfered the naked man's purse and uniform pockets. After they thieved all they could take, they escaped the tenement and made it to this room which served as a makeshift hideout.

Also inside the room now were three other youth including Ania, who was now fast asleep in the corner - his best friend, Amos, who was a slim, dark-haired youth from Cracow; and Amos' companion, Franco, a Polish, mean-eyed young man. Franco was a few years older than they were and liked to venture into the ghetto to buy cheap goods from the desperate Jews who filled the streets. Tomas stared at the starred armband that Franco was wearing then cocked his head and studied the young man,

wondering at his bravery.

    Franco had always made him uneasy. It was not the

scavengeristic nature of his ways – that Tomas admired especially

since he, himself, had now become an excellent forager. He did not

see Franco's venturing into the ghetto as an exploitation of their

vulnerability, but as an attempt at survival – an instinct that he,

himself, also knew all too well. But he did not trust Franco,

especially today as he listened to him laugh while describing to

Amos the entertaining events of his morning. He was absolutely

tickled pink as he spoke of a Christian being shot dead outside the

gate for throwing a loaf of bread over the wall.

    Amos turned and looked over to Tomas and his eyes

pleaded with his friend when he noticed the glint of anger in his

eyes. Tomas stared down at his hands and clenched his fists

causing Franco to stop laughing at once, feeling the tension as it

stood thick between himself and Tomas. Amos and Franco got on

well, so Tomas tolerated the grimy young man, but he didn't like

him – not one bit.

"Lighten up, Tomas. I'm just having fun." Franco jokingly held his hands up as if to ward off oncoming blows.

"What is the fun with a man being shot dead?" Amos asked with an irritated sigh.

"Oh, come on. What have they done for you?" Franco retorted and rested his hands on his knees and stared eagerly back and forth between Tomas and Amos. "Did they say, no, don't quarantine the Jews from the rest of the population? Don't rob them of their life's work, of their dignity – don't treat them like dogs. Did they?" He licked his lips and waited impatiently for an answer. "The answer is no. They got their shit together and hauled ass out of here so that you good folks could be packed in like sardines."

He announced this with a solid tap of one finger on the brim of his tattered, black cap and carried a look of triumph on his pale, whiskered face that made Tomas so sick that he tensely exhaled and tried to check his anger because he wanted to wrap his hands around Franco's smug head and dislocate his jaw.

In the year since Poland had been invaded, Tomas had

hardened in his young age. Acts of violence no longer startled him and he had begun to become accustomed to havoc. He marveled at the boyishness of his past thoughts – even smiled sympathetically at the Tomas that he once was.

He stood up now and adjusted the roll of salami and other goods that Amos had bound around his midsection with bandages, and then pulled his thin jacket closed, feeling the weight of the two potatoes that he carried in either pocket and the small bag of sugar and coffee that he had been able to obtain for his father. He would move stealthily through the ghetto and make his way back to his family with the smuggled food – feeling pride that he was defying the Nazis by refusing to live on the measly rations of food that they allowed them.

As he bid Amos goodbye, he deliberately excluded Franco all together then made his way out of the dilapidated store, carefully searching the semi-dark streets for the SS. They were known to come upon Jews suddenly, jumping out of trucks and attacking them with batons for no reason at all, and he had become adept at avoiding the gendarmes that strolled the ghetto maliciously twirling their rubber batons.

Unlike most inhabitants of the ghetto, including Amos, Tomas' family had thus far managed to remain alive and intact. Of course, the effects of war had touched them as it had others around them, and as a result, Miriam had slipped into a world of non-reality and Tomas doubted that his mother would ever return to her normal self. Gideon sometimes groaned with disappointment when he tried to speak to his wife only to have her respond to him with nonsensical babble.

Avigail, on the other hand, had become quiet and withdrawn with resentment for her present situation. She only spoke when she had to and her voice was always tinged with agitation. Even Tomas could not seem to draw her from her misery and he oftentimes found her staring forlornly, but thoughtfully, at the dirty, white armband that she so hated. The men remained tactful and resilient and Tomas, a feisty, wild-eyed youth, took to the Warsaw streets daily in search of whatever useful things his family could use, and in that way he was able to keep an ear to the ground for news from the Aryan world.

Tomas pulled his cap low over his eyes and moved swiftly along the street, expertly avoiding beggars and hungry eyed, dingy vagabonds. Even with his cap low, Tomas was still keenly aware of his surroundings. As he made his way, he slowly approached a woman who stood crouched on the curb with two small, crying children and as he passed he averted his eyes from her pleading, tearful gaze and cut his heart and ears off to the wails of her children as he quickly skirted past them.

A year ago a scene such as that would have made him empty his pockets of the food he secretly carried. He would have at least given her the potatoes to make soup, but he knew that she would only keep adding water until it thinned to nothing, and eventually, she and her children would again cry from hunger. In his mind, he was convinced that with or without his help, they would starve; that eventually he would pass this way again and one of the small, dirty children – maybe even the mother herself – would be missing. For Tomas, reality had sunk in long ago and he knew from experience that it was now every man for himself.

As he approached the tenement where his family now lived

in a crowded room with three other people, he cupped his gloved

hands to his mouth and blew into them, letting his warm breath

heat his hands through the holes in the ragged material. He

bounded the stairs on legs that were still strong and made his way

to their small, crowded apartment. When he walked in, his family

hardly acknowledged him and he quickly surveyed the cold room

as he entered and counted the people there.

Everyone was bundled up in layers of clothes and holey

sweaters – everyone except Miriam who had stripped down to just

her thin dress and boots. She smiled widely at him and winked as

he plopped down on the floor beside Gideon and emptied the

contents of his pockets. As he had known, Gideon was elated at the

sight of the coffee grounds and displayed them proudly to Jakob

who seemed more interested in the roll of salami.

"Beef or swine?" He asked Tomas sharply and stared at

him steadily under bushy, gray brows.

"Pork, uncle. It was all I could get."

"Good job, boy." Gideon told him and lightly tapped twice

on his son's forehead with the knuckles of a hairy fist. "If he's hungry, he'll eat it."

Jakob scowled at Gideon and started to break the smoked meat apart and distribute it to just their family, avoiding the other intent, hungry eyes in the room. He then hid the rest for the family's later consumption.

As Jakob and Gideon rekindled their conversation, Tomas did not raise his head or interject except when queried, but otherwise, listened quietly to their exchange of words. The only light came from a candle that sat beside an aging, rickety man that they also shared space with. He had no family – had lost his only son to the Warsaw bombs, but Avigail felt obliged to care for him as she did her mother, and she and Jakob shared food with him despite Tomas' protests. Beside him there sat another woman and man that stayed in the apartment as well, but they sometimes went missing from time to time and the Yusef family did not know them well.

Feeling content and semi-relaxed as he sat there with his family, Tomas pulled his cap over his face and reclined against the wall, from time to time reaching into his pocket and tearing off a piece of salami with ragged fingernails to stuff into his mouth. He chewed with an almost mechanical motion, his jaws moving robotically as he swallowed the food without tasting it. He had ceased to enjoy flavor long ago and ate now out of necessity to stay alive. Over Jakob and Gideon's voices, he could hear Avigail trying to feed their mother, but Miriam would not cooperate and sat cross-legged near a makeshift pallet staring straight ahead with a blank expression on her face.

"They killed them all?" Miriam asked this calmly and so suddenly that even Tomas lifted his cap and stared at her.

The room was silent as Avigail and the other occupants of the room turned and looked at her with an incredulous look on their faces, wondering if this was one of the rare moments where sanity returned and she remembered herself. Those were the times that they did not let escape, knowing that they only had a matter of minutes to enjoy her, and they did not speak but stared at her in surprise that she had addressed them and waited for her next words. Even the old man, Mort, opened his eyes and looked over at her.

"Blindfolded them and led them down into the Kampinos and shot them. They even killed priests and teachers. The rest were drug off to the Pawiak prison."

She whispered this fiercely with a feverish look in her starving eyes and Tomas replaced his cap over his face and resumed his robotic chewing, knowing that Miriam was repeating a conversation that she must have overheard from Jakob and Gideon.

"The Polish priests." Avigail repeated quietly as she thoughtfully traced the blue star of her armband with a fingernail.

"The Polish, yes." Jakob answered and pulled nervously on the leg of his worn slacks.

"That is unbelievable. I still can't believe this is happening." Gideon shook his head in disbelief.

Tomas almost snickered beneath his hat. Everyone was still so surprised! Their expressions so incredulous! At first he wondered if they were blind – that maybe they didn't see what was going on around them, but now he knew that Miriam was most likely the sanest person in the room. It killed him to watch his father attempt to hold on to his dignity – his integrity – to no avail, and anger sometimes made his gut boil until he thought he would choke and he bit back a bitter retort to his father's awed confusion.

He had resigned himself to the fact that there was nothing left for him to inherit and his right to earn a living had been snatched away from him. All around them people were dying and his patience with everyone's "shock" had begun to wear thin.

"...yellow fever. That's why I don't go out." Jakob was saying.

"It comes from the lice." Miriam whispered from her place on the floor and gestured with a thumb towards Mort, who grunted loudly in protest.

This time, Tomas could not help himself from snickering aloud.

They all jumped at a loud banging outside the apartment and Tomas leapt stealthily to his feet and started for the door only to be stopped by Gideon.

"Who's there?" His father called out in a strained voice.

"Please. Avigail." A feminine voice responded from the

other side of the door and they all relaxed.

Avigail sometimes nursed the sick or elderly around the Quarter for trade, and people sometimes sought her out at the apartment at all times when they were desperate to save a loved one. Gideon opened the door to a small, frightened girl dressed in men's pants and a long coat. Avigail went to the girl, and after speaking a few whispered words to her, started out of the apartment behind her.

"I will go with you." Tomas said and started towards her.

"No, Tomas." Avigail turned towards him and held up an impatient hand, but tried to control the irritation in her voice. "I am only going across the courtyard. I will return shortly."

She turned and followed the girl out of the apartment, but even after the door closed, Tomas stood there staring at the cracked, white washed wood with an uneasy, queasy feeling in his stomach.

"Come sit down, Tomas. She will return as always." Jakob called out to him.

Tomas stood at the door a moment longer and thought of

going after her. He didn't know exactly where she was going after

all, but if he followed her, she would lecture him for being

overprotective – for not giving her the opportunity for privacy. He

removed his cap and ran a hand through his hair then went and

resumed his seat next to his father.

He leaned against the wall then and laid his head back,

eyes open, and met Mort's emotionless stare. As the minutes turned

into hours, Miriam climbed onto her pallet and fell fast asleep

while Jakob and Gideon talked long into the night. Tomas dozed in

and out then, listening to their deep voices as they conversed, but

once Gideon and Jakob dozed themselves then fell into a deep

sleep, the room was silent and Tomas dreamt…

He was back in Kazimierz on the swings at the playground.

He was young – nine or ten maybe – and he was alone in the park

which was odd because he heard the chatter of many voices

speaking nearby but he didn't see anyone, so little Tomas ran in

the direction of the sound of human prattling. As he rounded the

corner nearest to old Mr. Rubenstein's candy store, he noticed a

huge gathering of people lined up and down the long street wearing their finest clothes. Jewels glittered at the ears of the handsomely dressed women and Mr. Isaacs had even taken out his antique walking stick with the solid gold handle.

Wondering what the occasion was, Tomas began to cross the street and head for his parents who stood nearby chatting with the tanner, but as his foot stepped down from the curb and into the street he stopped and turned, hearing shouting behind him.

Avigail stood on the stairs of a nearby porch wearing a yellow dress singed with soot. She waved her arms erratically and screamed at him then pointed back toward the crowd, and to Tomas' horror, there were now thousands of people all pointing and glaring at him with starving, ill-crazed eyes, and one by one, an orange-blue flame began to burn at their feet and spread quickly through them only to engulf their bodies in a great ball of searing fire. As they howled with the torment of being burned alive, Tomas fell to his knees in the middle of the street and wept while pounding the pavement beneath him with a small, bloodied fist...

He jolted awake in the darkness and sat momentarily

disoriented as the horror of the dream wore off. He wished that the candle had not burned out. Had he been asleep that long?

As he recovered from the nightmare, he wiped the sweat from his brow with his sleeve and waited for his heart rate to slow. All he could hear around him was the familiar, despondent bawling from the streets and the breathing of the people that surrounded him, but as he counted their bodies in the darkened room, he became nauseous when he came to the realization that Avigail was not among them.

Thirty-two days later

In the first few weeks after Avigail's disappearance, Tomas had gone literally mad searching for her. Grief-stricken, Gideon was convinced that she had been taken in a round-up and shipped to a labor camp, but Tomas did not believe that was the case. There was not one person who had seen a transport come through the ghetto the night Avigail went missing. If Jews had been taken off of the street then people would certainly be talking about it, and he and Avigail were known in the community. Someone would definitely come forward and tell him that they'd seen or heard of her being taken.

Daily, his eyes searched the faces of females that passed him on the street in hopes of seeing the small girl that had lured Avigail away. It seemed that she had simply dropped off the face of the earth as well, and Tomas could not forgive himself for letting Avigail go alone. When he thought of all the bad things that were certainly happening to her, he felt a rising sorrow that always settled into overwrought panic and he would nearly go mad searching for her. He stayed out longer these days, unable to cope with the pain that his family suffered because of the loss of Avi.

When Gideon had first realized that she was missing, he had tried desperately to remain optimistic; had went out on his own to search for her, sometimes not returning himself for days at a time. Jakob, on the other hand, was silently cynical.

Eventually, Gideon grew weary of himself and Tomas returning without his only daughter, and now Jakob was forced to keep watch over both Gideon and Miriam because once reality set in, Gideon collapsed on his backside and sobbed uncontrollably, rocking there with his mouth agape and tears running down his weathered cheeks.

The anguish of loss had finally settled over the family like a deep, dark smog and the expectation of desolation settled into their bones and they finally lost the last remnants of hope that they had clung to for so long.

Tomas sometimes struggled awake at night grasping his throat feeling as if he were being suffocated by thick, acrid smoke. On other nights, he would awaken to the sound of his uncle pacing the floor in his bare feet.

One such night, Tomas turned over on a thin pallet where he lay on the floor and flipped onto his left side in an attempt to alleviate the pain in his sore right hip. He had been startled by a momentary spark of light and then relaxed when he smelled tobacco burning. Jakob sat in the dark on the opposite side of the room near Mort, and the two men passed a rolled cigarette back and forth between them. For the first time in weeks, Tomas laughed quietly, knowing that his uncle had taken a tour of his coat pockets and found the now stale smokes.

Jakob's voice trembled with emotion as he spoke. "Maybe she was murdered for her ration card."

Tomas' smile faded in an instant and pain stabbed at his heart until it felt as if it were bleeding into his stomach.

"The boy looked everywhere for her?" Mort asked, and took a hit from the cigarette and Tomas watched as the flame illuminated his eyes and smoke drifted from his nostrils.

"Yes." Jakob whispered. "How could she just disappear like that?"

Tomas squeezed his eyes shut and swallowed as hot, frustrated tears pooled in his ear.

"Maybe she escaped." Mort said hopefully.

"How would she get over a ten foot wall by herself, Mort?" Jakob snapped sardonically, as if he had resigned himself to the surety of Avigail's demise and wanted no argument to the contrary. "I don't think so."

"She knows the language. Maybe –"

"No. She looks like a damn Jew. No way." Jakob took one last hit from the cigarette then smashed the butt into the floor and extinguished the flame. "She's dead. I can feel it."

His voice broke as he stood and he pulled his blanket tightly around his shoulders and sighed heavily, attempting to fight off grief pangs but was unable to control his emotions and turned with a sob and shuffled heavily from the room.

Tomas continued to search for Avigail even months after she disappeared. All over the Quarter he searched, leaving no stone unturned. Even his friends kept an ear open for any news of Avigail though they knew that sometimes people simply vanished – that sometimes the Nazis took them away never to return.

As the summer ended, conditions in the ghetto became even more unbearable. Debris and trash littered the streets. Beggars lay on the ground starving, too weak to move. The problem of overcrowding would be gradually solved by the dropping dead of people around them only to become crowded again with new deportees.

He had been walking nearby the gate – had then turned back and moved again throughout the Quarter with a faded photo of his sister, hoping to find a lead on what had happened to her, but searching for her had forced him to look with open eyes at the degradation and suffering that surrounded him. Those that did not have the ingenuity or shrewdness to survive did not eat, and as the Warsaw Quarter's inhabitants died in record numbers from disease and mind numbing, soul gnawing hunger, families too poor to pay for burial expenses stripped their dead loved ones naked and then left them in the street with newspaper covering their face to await the corpse cart.

The sight of the desperately hungry crowding around the soup kitchens, their bare feet digging into the wet, filthy earth beneath them as they eagerly awaited the watered down fare hardened Tomas' heart even more. He didn't want to see them – wanted to close his eyes to their misery. It agitated him to look at them.

The adults, though emaciated and a shame to behold, were not what held his attention as he walked the streets, and the sympathy that he felt for them was almost non-existent. He felt that soon they would be blessed with death and their agony would end

– this was their fate.

But the children – the suffering of the children bothered Tomas no matter how hard he tried to ignore it. They slept alone in the streets dressed in rags or leaned up against walls for support because their weak, swollen legs would not hold them. The bony little knees of some and the haunted, glazed over expression in the eyes of starving babes made his heart feel as if it would explode, and he and Amos would secretly sneak food to those they could without being detected, morosely walking by and stooping discreetly to tuck bread or dried meat into their small hands.

For weeks, those hands had tortured his sleep relentlessly, and he suffered the same recurring nightmare where he stood in the midst of a huge field where heaps upon heaps of tiny hands and feet putrefied in the sun. No arms, no legs, but thousands upon thousands of miniature, decaying fingers and toes for as far as his eyes could see.

He had been lucky – had stumbled across treasure in a crowded wasteland. That was how he had encountered Major.

Because at first there had been two…

There had been two children that hovered together in the same doorway day after day and gradually over time, as was normal, they slowly began to deteriorate – their small eyes were cast in shadows, their small backs bent, their cheeks hollowed out as they wailed aloud to no avail. No one stopped to help them, and eventually, they took on the deathly pallor that meant their time was almost at an end.

But now there was only one...

The frail boy did not lie in the doorway as usual, but on the cement instead in somewhat of a fetal position. As passerby somberly stepped over and around the nearly expired child, Tomas stood to the side and watched the small boy's back faintly rise and fall, waiting for the last breath to pass through him. Rags covered his small body and were even wrapped about his small feet and tied with rubber bands. Without thinking, Tomas walked over to the boy, stooped and scooped the pitiful, weightless form into his arms and walked away, deciding that the child would be welcome to Avigail's portion.

That day, and at the time unknowing to him, Tomas struck

up a relationship that proved to be invaluable with an orphan boy whose father had been carried off to the prison in Pawiak never to return and whose mother had taken ill and died, and whose sister had died only days before. As he nursed the feeble boy back to health, he listened to the child's tale of woe and decided that day that he would never again complain about the unfairness of his own situation.

Major, a blue eyed, brown-haired boy of ten years was extremely intelligent and loved Tomas from the moment that he lifted him from the street and whispered for him to breathe. He didn't remember nearly dying there on the ground, but he did remember that after Mina left him his strength had washed right away. The very instant he awoke – the moment his eyes fluttered open, he said he did as he had done every morning since his mother died and reached for Mina's small hand, but when he grasped it, he said that it had been too stiff, too still, and he had known what was wrong without looking at her. In his own words, he said that his heart broke again and again - that Mina had taken his strongness with her.

For Tomas, the beauty of it was that he was caring for a child that could fend for himself – with a little help, of course, for little Major had been forced to take care of he and his younger sister all on his own, and Tomas spoke to him in whispered tones about the worth in his small size because he could disappear through openings in the wall and out onto the Aryan side where he could carry messages, but mostly, where he was good at snatching bags of groceries and other goods from unsuspecting pedestrians as they walked the street.

"Why don't you go through the wall anymore?" Tomas had asked while he fed the boy a bowl of bean soup.

"They don't pay." Came the hoarse, child voice. He lifted a mangled hand to his wet nose and wiped with three of his remaining fingers. "And I couldn't leave Mina anymore. She got hurt last time."

In the past, he said that he would bring food in to the ghetto's inhabitants as a way to care for himself and Mina – food or medicine even from a stolen purse for someone's sick relative in exchange for somewhere safe to sleep. But there were instances when people didn't deal honestly with the small, vulnerable boy and he would most times be left in a worse position than he had started.

As time passed, Major's health improved and life and vigor returned to his small body. He was overly energetic, bouncing off the walls even, and to amuse the older boys, Major would dance and sing and crack jokes to Amos' utmost delight. Being an orphan himself, Amos took instantly to Major and agreed with Tomas that the boy was worth more than he ate. They drew lots and Amos won the right to keep him at the hideout as opposed to sending him to the crowded tenement with Tomas.

Amos got him shoes and clothed him and Tomas waited patiently until one day weeks later Major decided on his own to slip through the gate. After then, Major was never cheated again. People of the ghetto were forced to deal with Tomas or Amos when bartering, and Major stuck close to them and none of them suffered the hunger pangs that at times in the past had kept them up at night. Major got so adept at making it over the wall and back with goods that he would go several times a day, even being crafty enough to sneak past Tomas and Amos when they forbade him to go out again.

Today, Tomas and Amos made their way out of the hideout and then down Niska St. toward the gate. They walked with their heads downs and their hands in their pockets, silent as they went. Every so often, Amos would turn in a half circle and scan the street to be certain that they weren't being followed. Times like these kept them on edge. If they were caught smuggling goods into the Quarter they would be shot, and Tomas worried that Major, who's courage he did not doubt, would be sent off to a labor camp to die from exhaustion as well as starvation.

Tomas could only rely on the news that reached his ears and his own common sense told him that the Nazis weren't starving them in the ghetto only to serve steak dinners in a labor camp.

As they approached their meeting spot, they saw Major standing with a group of children who were searching their loads and bartering together, and Tomas laughed at the comical bunch as they squabbled, curious to see what they had found.

This was one of the ways in which Tomas and Amos were able to obtain cash and other valuables that they stashed for future use, and in this way, Tomas was able to make his first loan.

It happened purely by accident. He had been sitting in his usual corner of their hideout with Amos and two other young men in their gang, John and Joseph, sixteen year old twins. Both boys were tall, lanky, pimple-faced thieves, but reliable and trustworthy as far as Tomas was concerned.

Joseph and John were loyal to Tomas and Amos. As long as they had worked with them they ate, and sometimes in excess being that Tomas was not stingy and would spread things as evenly as he could between them all. As the group conversed, Tomas did not speak, but quietly listened to the voices around him as he watched Amos chain smoke. It had come to his ears something like this...

Adam Meyer, a member of the Jewish police force, owed a gambling debt to a Polish gangster that was due to be paid at noon the following day. Why Adam had taken the steep bet from the conniving Pole no one knew, except that Adam said he had been convinced that the win was a sure thing. The only thing anyone could say for certain was that this hoodlum would kill Adam if he didn't show up the following afternoon with 200 zloty – a figure that everyone knew Adam couldn't accomplish in so short a time.

So although Amos protested vehemently, thinking it a bad deal to call attention to themselves, within an hour Tomas had a desperate, perspiring Adam Meyer sitting before him ready to hand over his mother to save his own life. He did not bother to ask where Tomas had gotten the money or how, but accepted it gratefully with a promise to repay and Joseph smirked at the man in disgust but kept his mouth closed while Tomas placed twenty-five percent interest on the loan due and payable in two weeks, and Adam Meyer, petrified, relieved man that he was, thankfully accepted Tomas' offer and left the building with humble, downcast eyes.

From then on, Tomas earned himself the reputation of making fair loans, but of being swift and sure in doling out violence when cheated. He was known to carry a stone-faced, irritated expression on his young face and his demeanor was hard as concrete. No one fouled him – ever.

But his hard demeanor abandoned him that dreadful summer of 1941, and nineteen year old Tomas and his small family were again shattered.

It was a Sunday morning and Tomas had been home in the raggedy, overcrowded tenement with his family. He and Jakob had just returned from hiding a small bundle of cash and valuables, and they headed back to the small room where they lived to finish a meal of boiled potatoes and rice. Gideon sat quietly in one corner of the room attempting to sew rags together to tie around his bare, calloused feet, now finding shoes intolerable on his cracked soles.

Tomas had settled down next to his mother with sugared potatoes and attempted to coerce her into eating, which she still refused to do on a regular basis. Her dark, vacant eyes had stared at him without actually seeing him, and Tomas had longed to hear his mother speak his name and acknowledge his presence.

"Mom." He whispered to her and snapped his thick fingers in front of her eyes, hoping to break her from her world of escape.

Miriam did not respond but continued staring out around him and quietly mouthed an endless babble of words that he could not make out.

"Mom." He spoke to her again, this time grabbing her tightly about the shoulders and forcing her to look at him, which she finally did, and smiled. Thrilled, he smiled in return and waited hopefully for recognition to register in her haggard, drawn features.

"Avigail." She called quietly.

"Avigail?" He repeated after her through an instant of heart wrenching pain. He nodded at her, elated that she was speaking to him.

She sneakily looked about the room then leaned in and whispered to him. "Avigail and the baby?"

Baby? What baby? Tomas stared at his mother in shocked confusion wondering if this was just mere crazy talk. He turned to his father to see if he had heard, but Gideon continued his sewing, his brow etched deep in thought as he tried to complete his task.

Tomas turned back to his mother and she widened her eyes

and lifted a pale finger to her lips and shushed him. Her eyes burned into his own as she silently warned him to keep her secret.

"What baby, mom?" He whispered.

"A little itty-bitty baby." She informed him with a nonchalant shrug then got up and walked out of the room.

In stunned confusion, Tomas jumped to his feet and followed her until he realized that she was going to relieve herself, and unable to wait patiently for his mother to finish, Tomas took the opportunity to rush back to find Jakob.

"Uncle," he started, coming into the room and kneeling on the floor to shake awake a dozing Jakob.

"What, what!" The slumbering man said grumpily, peering at Tomas out of one agitated eye.

"Did Avigail have a fellow?"

Gideon looked up from his mending with a sharp turn of his head and squinted his bleary eyes at Tomas.

"You mean after Rye? No. My Avigail was a respectable young woman." He replied tersely and frowned, waiting for an explanation.

"I know, Papa." Tomas ran an irritated hand through his hair. *"I'm only asking because Mom said –"*

"Oh, hosh posh." Jakob grumbled and rolled over again. *"Miriam doesn't know her head from her –"*

Then the screams came – loud and piercing – searing Tomas' soul like a sharp, serrated knife cutting through warm butter. Coming from below – from outside – and even before the men leapt to their feet, Tomas slumped painfully against the wall, knowing that Miriam was gone. The same black feeling washed over him as he had felt the night of Avigail's disappearance, but this time there was no dreadful feeling of the unknown because the evidence lay sprawled out in the courtyard beneath them bloody and disfigured.

Miriam had wandered from the three room apartment where they lived and had ventured floors up, entering a filthy apartment where most of the inhabitants had perished weeks before. She had made a path through the trash filled room and finally stopped in front of a broken window, cutting her feet with shards of glass that littered the floor. Miriam had climbed up into that window in an almost certain moment of utter insanity, and

with a lack of fear, walked the edge of the window sill leaving

bloody footprints behind her.

But he had just spoken to her...

Tomas stood in the courtyard over his mother's broken

body and with his eyes warned onlookers not to approach and

tried desperately to ignore the loud, tortured screams of a woman

who had seen Miriam fall. He struggled to hold his composure and

stood hard-faced as his father, severely shaken with grief, knelt at

his mother's side. Large tears fell from his eyes and rolled down

his face in heavy streams and he looked helplessly up at Tomas as

if begging him to help him – to please take a portion of his hurt.

***

Amir closed the book and sat in silence as Ava sat on the

edge of the bed and wiped her eyes with a Kleenex.

"I didn't know he went through all that." Amir said quietly

them removed his glasses and rubbed his fatigued eyes.

"He never said anything to you?"

"No. They didn't talk about it. I mean, I knew by the tattoo that he had been through it but –" Amir stopped speaking and his eyes began to water.

Ava pulled another napkin from the box and blew her nose then handed a Kleenex to Amir. When she once again had herself under control, she climbed back beneath the covers and took the journal from him.

Ava again found their place then took a deep breath. "There's more about your mother. Okay?" She asked, making sure that he was ready to keep going.

When Amir nodded, Ava reached over and gently patted his thigh then began to read from the pages.

CHAPTER SIX

She jumped up and down again to see if her breasts would spill out of the scanty, lace confinement and shook her head when Michael whistled at her from the other side of the room.

"I can't wear this, Michael." Scarlett stood in the mirror and turned in a semi-circle then back again.

"I don't see why not. You have a great rack."

Michael sat at a vanity in her underwear and applied makeup to her pretty face while appraising Scarlett appreciatively through the mirror.

"You said you wanted something that wasn't too revealing. Well, this is perfect. You look great."

Scarlett turned and looked herself over again. The pants she absolutely loved – black silk hugged her hips and bottom and revealed curves that she had never realized she had and tied at her ankles with black, silk ribbons. Michael had also loaned her a pair of black high heels that made her feel sexy when she walked.

The bustier was the problem. Ivory lace hugged her slim waistline while tan, lace rosettes lined the edges of her cleavage.

She inhaled a deep breath then released it and watched the swell of her breasts press against the fabric. Michael had taken a hot iron to her hair and instead of a mass of unruly dark curls, Scarlett's hair now hung in bouncy, straight layers about her face and neck. Her brown eyes had been lined with a dark eyeshadow that gave them a smoky effect and her lips had been painted a naughty shade of red.

"Maybe I should wear my own clothes."

Michael shook her head as she stepped into her dress. "If Viola sees you downstairs in those knickers, she'll just die."

Scarlett rolled her eyes at the mention of Viola while Michael strode towards her in a forest green dress that slit at the side and exposed one shapely, cream-colored leg.

She stood in front of her with sparkling brown eyes but her gaze was serious. "Stay in the common areas. Okay?"

"Don't worry, Michael. I'll be fine."

Scarlett smiled in spite of herself as she moved with Michael through the smoke filled room. Men stopped speaking and eyed her with interest, even turning to look at her backside as she passed. Scarlett took a seat on a gray, leather chair and crossed her legs. Around her conversations went on, glasses clinked, and the sound of laughter met her ears.

"How are you, dear?"

Scarlett turned as Viola sat down beside her.

"I'm fine, Viola." Scarlett said slowly, suspicious of the smartly dressed woman.

"Well, don't be a wallflower. Why don't you mingle a little?"

"I'm fine right here, Viola."

"Here, dear, have a drink." Viola threw a hand into the air and gestured to a waiter who stood nearby holding a tray filled with glasses of champagne.

Scarlett took one and emptied it with a smack of her lips before handing it back to the waiter in exchange for a full glass. She walked away then, leaving Viola staring wide mouthed behind her.

While she held her third glass of champagne, Scarlett stood

by the piano and danced to the rhythmic melody that flowed from the piano keys. She felt good now. She was no longer nervous and when Michael came over and joined her, they happily danced the Charleston together while the crowded room clapped and cheered them on.

So Scarlett was not offended when he approached her as she sat at the bar sipping from her glass. She recognized him as one of the men whom Anna had been entertaining the first night that she had arrived at the house. He was much older than herself – much older than Viola even. Short and portly in a tailored suit with a thick, British accent.

"Gerald Fitzgerald, my dear."

He bowed as he approached her and held out a hand, and Scarlett, not wanting to be rude, placed one of her hands into his own and allowed him to brush hot, thin lips across her fingers. He smiled as he released her, revealing one large, gold tooth in the front of his mouth.

"What an exquisite creature you are." He exclaimed with another dramatic bow and placed a small hand over his midsection

and the other behind his back.

Unsure of what to say, Scarlett gave him a friendly smile and nodded.

"And what is your name?" With a look on his face that told Scarlett that he thought he was on the prowl, Gerald placed a foot on the base of the stool where she sat and leaned onto the bar beside her, winking coquettishly while his smile widened.

Scarlett held her breath for fear that she would burst into laughter. "Scarlett. I'm Scarlett."

"Scarlett." He repeated in a flirtatious, drawn out drawl. He growled then at her with a little rock of his head and leaned in closer to her. "And tell me, what is it that you want?"

"Beg pardon?" She asked, confused.

"Tell big daddy what –"

"Scarlett, I see you've found Gerry." Anna sashayed over to them and stopped to stare at Scarlett. Her surprised eyes looked her up and down then she smirked haughtily. "Well, look at you."

Scarlett opened her mouth to retort, but Anna cut her off and addressed Gerald.

"Gerald, how are you and Scarlett getting along?"

Anna, always feisty and decadently beautiful, flipped her perfectly manicured red hair as she spoke, and Scarlett narrowed her eyes with envy as Anna's bangs fell flawlessly back into place and feathered across her forehead. She arrogantly eyed Scarlett as she lightly dabbed her cigarette out in an ashtray, leaving behind a white butt that was stained with fuchsia lipstick.

Gerald felt the sense of derision directed toward Scarlett from the beautiful, blue-eyed woman, and he enjoyed being privy to it. He loved a good catfight. "Oh, just fine, Anna. I was just –"

"Gerald, you would not believe who Scarlett is acquainted with." Anna interrupted with wide-eyed innocence and stared expectedly at Gerald, waiting for his curiosity to pique, so Scarlett sat back and waited, knowing that Anna had something up her sleeve.

"Who's that?" Gerald's grin remained.

Suddenly changing course, Anna flipped her hair again and turned to Scarlett. "Dear Scarlett, has Gerry had an opportunity to tell you what he does?"

Scarlett did not respond but held Anna's wicked glare and waited. Gerald felt the tension thickening between the women. It was as if for them the music in the room had stopped and everyone else had up and left.

"Well, our Gerry here is one old villain. That's what he is." Anna said and leaned over Gerald and placed a kiss on the top of his shiny, almost hairless dome.

"Oh, stop it, Anna. I am only a businessman. Plain and simple." He said, hanging his thumbs from his waistband as he continued to smile flirtatiously at Scarlett.

"Oh, it's true. He runs a hard-nosed crew that nobody dares mess with." Anna purred.

Gerald smiled in spite of himself and rocked smugly on the balls of his feet.

"Like that guy over there." Anna said saucily, and they followed her gaze to where a rough looking man stood at the door with his hands behind his back.

He was tall and broad shouldered and sported a thick, white scar that started at his brow and extended to the corner of his mouth. *Mabel's friend,* Scarlett thought.

"That's just Howie." Gerald said nonchalantly with a wave of his hand.

"Well, I once saw Howie break a man's back just like that." Anna snapped her fingers to emphasize her words and held Scarlett's gaze again, and Scarlett wondered why she was keeping her in suspense – playing cat and mouse with her.

"Oh, that's what I was going to say, Gerry." Anna turned back to Gerald. "Tomas Yusef and Scarlett are acquaintances."

The lazy grin left Gerald's face then and was replaced by a hard, cold stare. Scarlett now believed Anna when she said that he was a villainous individual.

"They've only just met, but she lives in his house." Anna added.

Gerald turned again to look Scarlett over as if he thought he would find something new about her that he had missed the first time around. "You're joking!"

"I'm as serious as a heart attack. Isn't that right, sugar?" Anna turned innocently to Scarlett.

"Ah. She likes men with an air of surly indifference about them." Gerald laughed uncomfortably. *When Scarlett didn't respond, Gerald hitched his pants up and a quiet whistle escaped his thin lips.* "Now there's a man that knows how to get the truth out of a fellow."

"Well, she don't know nothing." Anna informed him spitefully. *"The girl is square with four corners."*

"Ah."

"Help me out, Gerry, will you?"

Anna's question clearly agitated him and he turned away from her. A deep frown furrowed his brow and he mumbled quietly to himself before asking, "Why don't you tell her?"

"She doesn't listen to me." Anna said smartly.

"Nah," Gerald said, shaking his head. *"I don't want anything to do with it."*

"Look at her, Gerry."

And Gerry did look at her – such a lovely face and healthy, olive complexion. Her beautiful brown eyes were surrounded by long, dark lashes, but narrowed now as they stared at him questioningly. Those innocent, alluring eyes.

Seemingly stressed, Gerald turned to the bartender and ordered a Scotch on the rocks, and as he drank, he again mumbled to himself.

Curious and thinking that she would never have another opportunity such as this, Scarlett ignored Anna and turned in her seat to face the now fidgety man. "Mr. Fitzgerald?"

He turned to her and smiled. "You seem like a very bright young woman."

"Thank you." Scarlett said, trying to hide her impatience.

"History is very important. Do you know that?"

"I don't know what you mean, sir."

He stared at her intently now and Scarlett knew that what he was about to say to her would be very important.

"Well, considering the company you keep, I simply figured that you might know a little bit about history." Gerald turned around to look for Anna before his eyes nervously surveyed the room. "You can tell a lot about a person from where they've been." He mumbled this softly, almost as if he were speaking to

himself.

"Mr. Fitzgerald?"

"For instance, the ancient Persians contributed a lot to history." He turned suddenly and pointed a short, stubby finger at her "Have you ever heard of the boats?"

"Mr. Fitzgerald, I don't –"

"I see that I have you at a disadvantage. Here's a history lesson – the Persians were masterminds when it came to inventing macabre means of torture to inflict on their fellow human beings. One was a method by which you take a man and constantly force feed him an abundance of milk and honey. This is known, of course, to cause terrible bouts of diarrhea.

You strip him naked and coat him with the sweet concoction - his genitals, even his face. Then you take that man, confine him in a boat of sorts and send him to float on a standing pond.

Although there are others," he turned and stared meaningfully at her, "who prefer staying with their victim throughout the ordeal, so they simply take the unfortunate creature out to a deserted field at the time when spring and summer thrive and they never encounter interruption."

He again quickly surveyed the room but was encouraged to continue by a stiff jab from Anna's elbow.

"Do you know, Scarlett, the number of insects that are attracted to honey and human waste?"

Scarlett refused to believe - couldn't believe this nonsense - and climbed down from the bar stool and prepared to walk away only to have Anna step forward and block her path. As the party went on around them, Anna folded her thin arms over her silk clad chest and her blue eyes glittered with envy as she eyed Scarlett.

From behind them, Gerald continued to speak with a faraway tone to his voice. "Can you imagine, Scarlett, being confined in a box with only your head exposed while your flesh is covered with stinging, biting insects? Can you imagine the agony of having maggots swarming in and around your asshole while you sit and rot in your own excrement, unable to move?

Hell, I've heard tell of a man's entire head being covered with flies. And when it's all over, it's as simple as lighting a match *and walking away." Gerald's face had turned bright red and beads of sweat covered his forehead. He seemed to Scarlett to be unbearably nervous. "I see that you have a vivid enough picture in your mind already, so I will keep any additional lessons to myself. Excuse me, ladies."*

As Gerald walked away in one direction, Scarlett sidestepped a smirking Anna and ran from the room feeling sick and very frightened all at the same time.

Early the next morning, Scarlett snuck quietly into the house. She stood still and listened for any sound from the upper floor then crept silently up the stairs to her room. Her heart pounded as she went, and uncertainty gnawed at her insides until she felt as if there was a hole being burned into her stomach.

She hadn't wanted to believe Gerald – had tried to forget his words, but deep down she knew that what he had said was true. Michael had not wanted her to return to the lonely, cold house but Scarlett had been determined to gather her belongings. Tomas was rarely home anyway and she felt that her chances of getting in and out undetected were good.

As fast as she could, she packed her things and headed again for the door. She breathed a sigh of relief as she descended the stairs and then cringed as the door suddenly swung open and Tomas entered, smiling broadly when he noticed her standing there.

They stared at one another for a moment – him starting to frown at the fearful, confused expression on her face, and he shut the door behind him and locked it then moved swiftly towards her, and when his foot touched the steps, Scarlett backed away. She did not like the look in his eye – cold, yet possessive.

Seeing no other way of escape, Scarlett turned and walked back up the stairs to her room and he pursued her, moving so closely behind her that she stumbled nervously into the room, tripping over her feet and falling to the floor. Scarlett attempted to avoid his gaze as he leaned over and stared at her as if she were crazy.

"Are you looney?"

"I'm leaving, Tomas."

"No, you're not leaving, Scarlett."

"Oh, yes. I'm leaving." Scarlett jumped to her feet and stared at him defiantly.

She would not be bullied, she told herself, but as she tried to walk around him he stepped in front of her, refusing to let her pass.

"You are not leaving."

Scarlett met his eyes then. "Tomas, let me pass."

"Tell me, Scarlett, where have you been?"

She could tell by the way he was looking at her that he already knew. So what. "It's none of your business, Tomas. Let me pass."

"None of my business?" He grabbed her then by her collar and Scarlett gasped in surprise as she was lifted off her feet, and she held onto his strong forearms for support lest he choke her.

But as they stared into each other's eyes, Tomas was taken aback at her hostile glare, so accustomed was he to her adoration. It was as if she had completely shut him off from her heart.

"What's wrong with you?"

"Put me down." Scarlett said though she was unprepared when he abruptly set her upon her feet and she fell back onto the bed.

"You're not leaving, Scarlett." He said quietly, determined that she would back down.

"Or what? You're going to torture me?"

"What the hell are you talking about?" He exclaimed loudly.

"You know exactly what I'm talking about."

Tomas scratched his beard in agitation. "Hmm. Why don't you tell me where you were last night, Scarlett." Tomas situated himself between her and the doorway and obstinately folded his arms over his sturdy chest.

"I was at a party at a friend's house."

"At the hospitable, despicable house of Viola Little. Correct?"

Scarlett stared at him then as if he had two heads, but he did not care.

"Then you know Anna, right?" Scarlett shot at him with a

jealous, biting tone.

"I know Anna, yes. Is that what this is about?"

His eyes, now hopeful, thoroughly searched her own, but Scarlett shook her head and got up to pace the room.

"Are you a murderer, Tomas?"

Irritation tinged his voice though he tried to hide it, and he took a step toward her and narrowed his eyes. "Someone told you something, Scarlett. Tell me what."

Scarlett lifted her chin and returned his stare without blinking. "I will not say, Tomas. Now answer me."

She didn't expect him to say it but he did.

"Yes."

"Just like that, Tomas?"

"If I could keep it from you, I would, but it has come to you already. I will not lie."

"So you kill people?"

He forcibly exhaled then threw his hands into the air and leaned against the wall. "Not all the time." He answered and wondered if he seemed too nonchalant. "What do you want me to do, Scarlett?"

"Not hurt people, Tomas."

"Scarlett, I don't hurt just anyone." He shrugged his shoulders and looked around the room, desperately struggling to find the right words to appease her. "What can I say? I'm a sonofabitch, Scarlett. I can't help it."

Scarlett flopped down on the bed again. Another fine mess she had gotten herself into.

"What am I supposed to do?" He asked.

Scarlett almost laughed. He really seemed as if he didn't know what to do and he turned then and tried a different tactic.

"It's not that bad, honey."

"It is, Tomas."

"How, sweetheart?" He came and knelt in front of her and his eyes pleaded with her – those hard but honest hazel eyes.

Slowly his arms encircled her waist and he buried his face in the soft flesh of her abdomen and inhaled her scent. She sighed when the warmth of his exhaled breath fanned across her stomach through the fabric of her blouse and she could not help herself from leaning forward and running her hands down his shoulder blades and over his muscular back.

She could not leave him – would not.

"I would never hurt you, Scarlett." He whispered and pulled her closer to him.

She believed him. "What do you want from me, Tomas?"

"I want you to love me."

Scarlett's heart skipped a beat but she grinned and cradled his worried face in her palms, staring into his serious eyes while entwining her fingers in the coarse, dark-brown and red tinged hairs that covered his face. She sighed peacefully and rested her forehead against his own.

"I want you to marry me. Stay with me. Give me children." He whispered and pulled her closer to him. "Leave my business outside where it belongs and greet me kindly when I come home to you. Be my wife, Scarlett. Let me take care of you."

"I would always worry about you." She whispered. "Aren't you ever afraid?"

"No, sweetheart. Out there, I am the wolf."

Days passed before Tomas left her again, but not before he forbade her to go back to the large Victorian house to visit Michael. Long, lonely days turned into a week and Scarlett was left totally to her own devices. The third day she stood near the stairs facing the front door and sipped her coffee, wishing that Tomas would come home. She felt like she had simply been dropped there again like a sack of potatoes without any word and she felt like a plant – one of the plastic, too green kind.

The fifth day she did as he told her and shopped for furniture for the house – her house, he'd said. He wanted her to be comfortable; he wanted her to make a home for them.

Scarlett wanted him by her side, but as always, he was gone and she was alone. She stood in front of a floor model television set and hardly heard the salesman's pitch. All she wondered was, was this how her life would be? Would she only see Tomas for moments that simply did not last?

A week later when Tomas entered his bedroom, he was

welcomed by the sweet aroma of a naturally clean woman. He stopped dead in his tracks then and stared in surprise at Scarlett lying half-naked in his bed. She was sprawled across the coverlet on her back as comfortably as she pleased.

What was he supposed to do?

He reached behind him and pushed the door closed then inhaled again. His brain told him how she would taste and he savored the flavor of her on his tongue as he walked across the dark room and leaned over her sleeping form.

He hurriedly undressed, his eyes never leaving her, and climbed into bed beside her, eagerly pulling her warm body into his arms. He pulled her closer until his nose touched her own and pressed a hungry kiss to her lips.

Scarlett felt so warm in her sleep – like she was wrapped in a steel furnace.

"Where have you been, Tomas?" She asked and draped a smooth thigh across his bare hip, pressing her body as close as she could to his own and moaned as his grip tightened around her.

"What are you doing, Scarlett?" He whispered.

She told him with her mouth what she was doing – that she

had been yearning to run her fingers through the dark hair that

covered his hard, bare chest – to wrap her arms around his neck

and mold her body to his own so that he knew how much she loved

him.

"I told you, Scarlett, that you are welcome to any room in

the house." He said while his lust filled eyes looked down at her.

"Even yours, Tomas?"

"Especially mine." He whispered.

Tomas thought about all the fretting that he had been doing

about her night and day and here she was lying willingly in his

bed.

"Stay with me." Scarlett whispered with her lips upon his

own.

She kissed him then, full and warm on the mouth and

entwined her slender fingers in the coarse hairs of his beard. The

drapes were mostly drawn and only slim slivers of light escaped

into the room. It was dreary out and she could hear fat drops of

rain hitting the roof as Tomas turned her over onto her back and ran his hands over her body. She closed her eyes and arched her

back when his mouth brushed across the tender flesh of her throat

and she relaxed into him as his body pressed her fully into the soft

mattress and pillows beneath them.

She parted her legs and Tomas reached in between their

bodies and greedily cupped her vagina in his hand and softly

squeezed –

***

"Wait, wait! I don't want to hear this." Amir reached over

and started to turn the pages.

"Hold on, Amir." Ava pouted.

"I don't want to know that, Ava."

"Oh, that's okay, babe. Don't worry. I'll just read it quietly

to myself." Ava smiled mischievously and turned her attention

back to the pages before her.

"Why do you get to read it?"

"Shhh."

***

Tomas settled his weight over her and his mouth found the

hollow of her throat and Scarlett's heart pounded as his hands caressed her beneath the sheets. Gently, as his mouth placed soft kisses along her shoulders, he opened her up and spread both hands over the most tender part of her body and massaged her so slowly that she had to lift her hips into his searching fingers to relieve the pulsating throb there.

She groaned in protest when he removed his hands, but she could feel the hardness of his erection as it rested against the moist softness of her body, and instinctively, Scarlett rotated her hips against him, and as his tongue and lips trailed a hot path from her shoulder to the hard, dusky nipple that lay beneath the silk of her brassiere, he met her rotations and the hardness of his body pressed into her and Scarlett felt as if she were melting beneath him.

Confused, Scarlett's mind stalled as the back of her thighs came to rest on his shoulders and her eyes flew open, but when she attempted to scoot away, he aggressively pulled her back to him.

"No, Tomas. Wait."

"Trust me." He whispered.

Those soft words.

"What are you doing?" Her voice did not sound like her own. Her mouth felt dry and she tried to clear her fuzzy brain so that she could think of the right words to tell him – a way to tell him that she wanted him to touch her inside...

"First, you have to whisper to it." He said softly.
And he did – he did whisper and the feeling of his warm breath and soft mouth moving over her as he cradled her buttocks in his strong hands sent chills up her spine. But then he kissed her and she inhaled a sharp breath as her body turned to jelly. Between kisses, she felt the warm, wetness of his tongue circling and exploring her, and then he took her fully into his mouth and she suddenly felt hot all over.

Tomas groaned roughly as he kissed her - as a pulsating fire burned within her then exploded into millions of blissful, dizzying lights. But when her mind cleared, she realized that he was prodding at her for entrance to her body. An animal-like groan escaped his throat – guttural and gratified as he held her there while he searched her, and Scarlett gasped at the first pierce of pain and then her body began to stretch around him. She braced her hands against the hardness of his belly to calm the aroused strength in his hips and he tensed and closed his eyes, bending one of her legs at the knee while he held on tightly to one of her ankles, and Scarlett felt the hard muscles of his stomach tighten beneath her fingers as he fought for control.

Again he went at her - a little at first then back again - breaking past her body's barrier – in and out until she was able to take all of him, and Scarlett's eyes rolled back with pleasure and she wantonly lifted her hips to meet his own. He entwined his fingers roughly in her hair and she winced and her eyes flew open to meet his own.

"Look at me." He growled hoarsely.

Save for the satisfied sounds of their lovemaking and the rain hitting the windows of the house, the room was silent, and Scarlett watched his half-hooded eyes darken into a sensual, brown mist as their bodies strained and undulated together. Tomas groaned from deep within his throat and cradled her in his arms as he took her and Scarlett felt a certain power that she had never felt before and she experimented with him – provocatively moving her hips to find what gave him pleasure.

And he gritted his teeth and groaned into her mouth while his tongue searched for her own, and Scarlett found that the pleasure he gave her was overwhelming and she fought to keep her eyes open. It seemed that he touched every nerve inside of her - and outside even as his hands made their pleasurable exploration of her back and breasts, and she spread her legs open as far as they would go and let bliss overtake her.

Tomas would hold her body under his control as he lay with just the tip of his manhood inside of her then slowly enter her again, slowly burying himself to the hilt until the fire started within her anew – that pulsing, overwhelming pleasure that made her body quake and go weak, and Scarlett's own hips became eager as she rose against him when he held back from her.

Tomas shuddered as her slick, warm body gripped him too tightly, and when she moaned and her body quivered around him, he met his end. As his seed spilled inside of her, he joyfully endured the exquisite feeling of her silken legs wrapped tightly about him, her hips urgently rising and falling to meet his own, fighting him for possession of his –

***

"Ava!"

"What, Amir?" Ava held her hands out and raised her eyebrows in mock innocence. "I'm all done."

"I can't believe you read that!" Amir shook his head and stared at her as if she should be contrite, but they both knew that she was not.

She hugged the journal to her chest and pretended to swoon. "Amir, your father is so –"

"Ava!"

With an annoyed expression on his face, Amir snatched the diary from her and gave her his back, and Ava fell back onto the pillows and laughed wickedly to herself as Amir again began to read.

***

When it was over, they lay there an arm distance away from one another, elated as the feeling of urgency in their loins slowly subsided and the heaving of their chests eased with the gradual slowing of their heartbeats. Tomas was satisfied and sleepy and Scarlett was pleased and sore, and she turned and cuddled up next to him and together they snored.

Neither one of them had family to share their wedding day with, so Tomas and Scarlett went to the courthouse alone, and when the small ceremony was over, he carried her over the threshold of their home and up the stairs to their bedroom where they made love throughout the day, only stopping to sleep or laugh together while they pigged out naked on the bed.

As the months turned into a year, their love grew as did Scarlett's belly, and when Amir finally arrived, Tomas at first did not approach the hospital bed where Scarlett lay breastfeeding their son. Scarlett was not surprised. She knew her husband – knew that he would watch over them because that was how he loved.

He stood in the corner and stared as his son's tiny hand grasped her finger while his little eyes attached to her face. Tomas could not believe that the pair of them belonged to him. In an instant, he loved Amir just as much as he loved Scarlett, and he made a vow to them both that no matter what, he would make sure that they were always safe.

PART TWO

"As it is written: 'For your sake we are being killed all day long;

we are accounted as sheep to be slaughtered." - Romans 8:36

CHAPTER ONE

March 1942   *Warsaw District*

"Half is half, Adam. It was half when you took the money.
It's still half now."

Adam sat back in his seat and sighed. He was having a
hard time manipulating Tomas into seeing things his way.

He tried a different tactic. "Do you know what the cost of
potatoes is right now? I have three little ones to feed. My wife –"

Tomas sat forward in his seat and leveled his gaze upon
him. "You still have a family?"

Adam closed his mouth then, realizing that he was treading
on dangerous ground. Though much younger than his own thirty-
nine years, this young man had always given Adam the creeps. It
was the way he stared at a man – would step right up to him and
speak to him literally face-to-face, unblinking, and hungry-eyed
though it was obvious he ate well. The muscles in his forearms
rippled with each squeeze of a small, orange rubber ball that he

constantly clutched in his right hand...

The ball reminded Adam of the boy, Major. He had seen many times when Tomas would take the ball and bounce it off the energetic boy's head to get his attention. Major seemed to be the only person who was allowed to play games with Tomas. With everyone else he was unfriendly and stone-faced. Even now he stared at him with his eyebrows raised and awaited his response.

Adam sighed. "I lost my family – everyone except my wife and children."

Tomas sat back again and studied him with hard, observant eyes. "There you go, Adam. Luck is on your side."

"Okay, Tomas. Okay. Well, the reason I stopped by was I have some information that I thought you and Amos would want to hear about."

Tomas glanced over at Amos who reclined in a wooden chair on the opposite side of the room chain smoking as usual. He raised a hand into the air, gesturing for Adam to speak, and as he did, Tomas looked irritably around and noted to himself again how this particular room retained its dust no matter how many times he made Major sweep it. The walls had yellowed long ago and the paint on the bare, wooden floors had begun to chip and peel in the many places where the floor splintered. He leaned back in his chair and closed his eyes.

Adam was speaking of mass annihilation, and as always, Tomas couldn't seem to get his brain to register the rightness of the reasons why people around him were being forced into such pitiful debilitation, but the fact remained that they were tucked behind stone walls, hidden from the rest of the world – seemingly easily forgotten. They were now enemies of the state – that fact was clear, and the thought made him think of Avigail. It was definitely something that she would have said.

He inhaled deeply as the same sharp pain burned in his chest when he thought of her, and he waited and held his breath until the old ache subsided then forced himself to concentrate on Adam, and as he listened, he wondered at the veracity of the man's words and turned his head and looked over to Amos to gauge his friend's reaction.

"And you know this to be true?" Amos asked and lit

another cigarette. A deep frown creased his forehead.

"They're being gassed in vans."

Adam sat across from Tomas and held his hat in his hands. Dark shadows had set up permanent residence beneath his deep set eyes and his dry lips twitched nervously while he spoke.

"At first, they would take them out to the woods and make them dig their own graves, but shooting them was too slow and that sort of thing stresses the soldiers."

"The soldiers?" Amos' face twisted in disgust. "No shit."

"Well, they found another way." Adam cleared his throat. "It's faster to just gas them all together."

"The Gestapo, is it?" Tomas sat forward in his seat and met Adam's gaze while Amos stood up and paced the floor between them.

"The Einsatzgruppen."

"Where did you hear this, Adam?"

"From SS officers – well, that's where it started. I've heard it more than once from different places, Tomas, and just like everything else, I'm sure it's true." Adam cleared his throat and

slumped back into his seat then rubbed a hand over his tired face.

"The point is that it's only a matter of time before – well, you

know. But the offer still stands about getting out on a lorry. I can –

"

"Thank you for coming, Adam." Amos cut him off before he

could complete his sentence. There was no need. They all knew

what the bottom line was.

"You've been good to me – you and Amos." Adam said

with somber sincerity.

Though he had made a lot of money dealing with Adam,

Tomas did not offer a congenial response and neither did Amos.

They knew that Adam had been very beneficial for them over the

last several months - had made things easier for them to conduct

business throughout the community without police harassment, and

bribes had taken them a long way in the ghetto.

Tomas could afford to keep a clean room for his father and

uncle. He could even afford to send Jakob and Gideon to the cafes

where the elite dined – if they had wanted to go that is, but they

always refused, even when Tomas asked them to go if only to stay current with what was happening in the rest of Poland, but Jakob would coolly request a propaganda filled newspaper - when Tomas could get his hands on one - and Gideon snubbed his nose at the socialites.

Mort had died peacefully in his sleep shortly after Miriam died, and instead of leaving his body in the street as others did with their dead, they had waited to mournfully carry his aged body out to the handcart and gently place it beside the other dead who had also managed, through death, to find an escape from the labyrinth of mayhem that was the Warsaw Ghetto. Jakob had mourned his friend, and Tomas had grown melancholy with the thought that his uncle or Gideon would be next. He saw their condition as a curse and he wanted free of it.

The silence from the two young men seemed to make Adam uncomfortable and he stood and brushed his pants leg with large, stiff hands then replaced his hat atop his head. "I have to get going. Any pickups today?"

"No, Adam. There's only two and Joseph will pick them up later." Tomas said and watched as Amos shook Adam's hand *before seeing him to the door.*

"What do you think?" Amos asked once the man departed.

"I think it's past due time for us to go. Has Franco –"

Tomas was interrupted mid-sentence as Major came bounding through the door without knocking. As always, Amos was elated to see the boy and instantly drew him into a headlock and roughed him about.

"Where have you been, you little crumb snatcher?" He teased as he dug his knuckles into the back of Major's skull.

"Unhand me, you big oaf!" Major struggled and squirmed until he escaped, panting and red-faced. "I need to talk to you, don't ya know?" He frowned as Amos attempted to again creep upon him and he pointed a small, serious finger as if warning him to stay away.

"What is it?" Tomas asked, chuckling at the boy as his small eyes darted around the room in search of an escape route then bounced back to a sinister-looking Amos.

"Remember I was telling you I found a way out on the underground. Now we can get your old men to the other side."

Tomas' eyebrows rose in surprise. "Well, out with it then."

"I found it on my own – well, Jojo found it anyway. No one really knows about it." Major stared earnestly at Tomas and hoped that he would trust him.

Amos ground his cigarette butt into the floor with the bottom of his shoe then pulled another from behind his ear and lit it. "Jojo and his mother are gone now, right?"

Major nodded his head. "Through the underground, I tell ya." He said this in an awe-struck tone and his thin, brown eyebrows lifted in amazement.

"And how does it work?" Tomas asked, gently prodding Major for more information.

Major looked from Tomas to Amos then back again. "Well, Koch says – "

"Koch? Who's Koch?"

"The man I was telling you about, don't ya know?" Major explained impatiently. "I told you, he helped Jojo and his mother cross over on the underground."

"A German, Major?"

"Sure is."

"I doubt it, Major. Nobody wants the Jews." Amos' eyes squinted as he puffed at his cigarette and he shook his head in disbelief.

"It's true, Amos." Major said and sighed loudly with frustration. "Koch's house is where they start. Jojo is probably in the Phillippines by now."

"The Phillippines! Is that what he told you?" Amos' voice trembled and Tomas knew from experience that he was becoming angry.

"It's true, Amos. Jojo was my best buddy. I would know if something was going on."

Tomas bent at the waist until he and Major were eye level. He trusted the boy, but he didn't put it past a German to manipulate a child in order to gather information about rebellious Jews in the ghetto.

"Did he say anything about papers?"

"He said that you don't need papers. It's better that way even."

"You have got to be kidding me. Tomas, you're not falling for this are you?" Amos turned his head and spit on the floor as he was wont to do when agitated.

"Aww, Amos, he's not like the others." Major balled his fists at his side and glared at Amos. "I told you he just wants the money. He says he'll hide you as long as you need if you're paying."

"No way, Tomas. What's to keep him from taking the money and turning us all in. We'll be totally at his mercy." Amos nervously paced the floor of their hideout.

"Who else is there?" Tomas asked softly, seeing Major's apprehension at Amos' outburst.

"It's just Koch and another woman who's going on the underground too." Major's tone had lost its confidence and he nervously fingered the hem of his jacket whilst eyeing Amos from the corner of his eye.

Tomas smacked his knee to regain Major's attention. "That's it?"

Major's small head bounced vigorously up and down.

"Count me out." Amos said this outright without a tinge of regret.

"How much longer can we wait?" Tomas asked, turning to his friend.

Amos shook his head and stared at him as if he were speaking French. "I say we wait right here." Amos resumed his pacing. "We've survived this long – we can make it a little longer. Franco's uncle will have new documents for us all any day now."

"Bullshit, Amos. How long have we been waiting?" Tomas grew agitated at the mention of Franco. "He traipses through here every week and says the same thing, but never delivers. He has the money in his hand." Tomas loudly smacked his palms together. "What do we have?"

Amos gritted his teeth while Tomas waited for a response with his hands out.

"Where, Amos?"

"You can say what you want, but I say that we're better off in here behind these walls then out there living under a roof with Germans. I'm not closing my eyes around one – I'll tell you that

right now. You need a better plan."

Amos lit another cigarette and leaned against the wall with his hands in his pockets. He had made his position clear, but Tomas had more to consider than just himself and Amos, and the longer he stayed in Warsaw, the surer he was that his family would continue to drop like flies. He absolutely understood Amos' position, but after hearing Adam, he was all the more desperate to get away, and he would risk capture to escape the hell that he lived with now. The way he saw it, Gideon and Jakob were dead either way. If this Koch fellow tried to exploit their vulnerability then he would spend his rage on him before he met his own end. Tomas shrugged his shoulders. It was that simple.

"I don't have any documents, Amos, but I can still go with Koch. Don't make me go alone." Major's sad, deep blue eyes pleaded with him, but Amos ignored him and spoke to Tomas.

"I don't like it." Still skeptical and hard-faced, he held his ground.

"You won't even check?" Major exclaimed with an agitated look on his small face and both hands out at his sides.

"Don't raise your voice at me, Major." Amos scowled at the angry boy and pointed at him. "And I should break your butt for cavorting with that gentile anyway!"

"Yeah? What about you and Franco?" Major argued, placing a hand on his hip and standing his ground.

"That doesn't count." Amos told him straight-faced.

"I'm almost a man, Amos – you said so yourself. I've made my decision and I'm going." Major stuck his chest out and glared at Amos.

"And you know what's gonna happen, Major?" Amos said quietly. "They're gonna take your money and turn you in."

"But you said we were gonna go together, Amos." Major whined.

"And we will, me and you together, but not this way. It's not safe."

Tomas had never seen his friend beg before today and his gray eyes shone as he pleaded with Major to stay with him, but Major had already begun to stay out longer than usual in the past few weeks, and Tomas knew the stress that it caused Amos when

Major was away, but did not speak about it, knowing that his friend sometimes stayed awake at night waiting for the boy to return to him.

He had taken note of Major as well and had often wondered where he slept when he was gone for so long on the Aryan side of the wall. He had not mentioned this either because he saw the effect that living in the ghetto was having on the boy – so bad at times that he stared into space and bit his fingernails until they bled. What Tomas saw in those moments when the boy was lost in daydream reminded him of Miriam and he did not blame Major for wanting to go.

But Major was sad now as he stared down at his small feet. "Well, I'm going."

"Go then. I hope they make soap outta you." And as he stumped loudly from the room, Amos swore, and the door slammed into the wall behind him so hard that the doorknob fell and hit the floor with a loud bang.

Tomas grabbed Major by the collar of his jacket and pulled him to stand in front of him. Tears brimmed in the small boy's eyes and he constantly kept looking over his shoulder towards the door as if thinking of running after Amos.

"Are you sure, Major, that this is what you want to do?"

"It is, Tomas." Major turned to him and settled his piercing blue eyes on him. "There's a Jewish woman there who lost all her children..."

Tomas leaned back in his seat and studied the small boy, glad that the mystery of his unexplained disappearing acts was finally solved. He had somehow become attached to this woman who hid with the German.

"I was hoping that Amos would come with us." Major said then looked away guiltily.

"Major." Tomas waited for their eyes to meet. "I've just lost my mother too. Do you remember?"

Major's small head bounced up and down and he tried to blink back tears.

Tomas placed a hand to his own broad chest. "I'm a man, but I still miss my mother very much. You know, it's okay for you to care for this woman."

Tomas watched as the boy turned his words about in his head. "But I don't want Amos to think that I don't love him."

"A lot of bad things have happened to you, Major, and you're just a little boy, but," Tomas held up a finger, "you are a survivor. I knew it from the very first moment that I saw you. I will speak to Amos for you. Okay?"

Major stared trustfully at him while his small head bobbed up and down.

"Good. Now hug me then."

Major threw himself at Tomas and squeezed him as hard as his small but strong arms would allow.

"Okay. Run along before I give you a wallop."

Tomas balled a fist and shook it threateningly at the boy who grinned broadly and lifted his chin in playful defiance. As he made his way to the door, he did a somersault in the middle of the dusty, wooden floor and landed perfectly on his feet. Before he closed the door behind him, he gave Tomas a sly wink and then, as was now usual, he was gone.

Tomas did not speak as he and Amos made their way to the day's last pickup. When they had first set out, he had attempted to participate in conversation but he soon realized that Amos was trying to goad him into an argument, and so he had ceased speaking altogether. Tomas knew that his friend was upset and he thought it wise to wait a day for Amos to calm down before he spoke with him about Major, but Amos refused to allow his friend to back down and continually attempted to trap him.

"I mean, what do you think, Tomas?"

Amos threw his cigarette butt to the ground then irritably scratched at his stubbly beard. When Tomas did not reply, he turned an angry, gray glare upon him to signal that he expected an answer to his question, and Tomas shook his head then, unwilling to jump into the snare. He turned and walked backwards then beside Amos and scanned the semi-crowded street for Joseph and his brother. He spotted the two young men walking behind them on the opposite side of the street, and as always, John's eyes stayed upon his brother and he followed his lead even though they were several feet from one another. Tomas nodded to Joseph who returned his acknowledgement by cradling his right hand with his left, and cocking his index finger as if he held a gun, mock-fired at Tomas.

"I don't know why I'm trying to talk to you anyway. You've always thought that Major was more yours than mine because you found him." Amos said to him with a grim face.

Tomas turned again and faced the direction that they were walking in but still bit his tongue. He and Amos had been friends a long time and he knew that if he couldn't goad him into giving a wrong answer, then he would accuse him of something to bait him. Soon, if Tomas continued to ignore him, Amos would only address him as "motherfucker".

Feeling slightly amused, Tomas turned and stared innocently at him then said the magic words. "Leave him be. You always over react, Amos. Calm down."

"Over react? I'm over reacting?" His eyebrows rose and he held his hands out in frustration. "Are you crazy? Did you hear what he said?"

His voice had become shrill and Tomas bit his tongue to

keep from laughing.

"Calm down, Amos," he said. "Or you'll pee yourself."

"This is not a joke, Tomas."

"I know that, Amos, but everything is so one-sided with you. I'm telling you that you don't know the whole story."

"He's just a boy, Tomas."

"This is true, but he survived a long time on his own before we found him. He has learned a great deal being with us, and ultimately, it is his choice." Tomas turned and looked at Amos then. "How will you stop him? Will you hold him prisoner, Amos?"

Still stern faced and unwavering, Amos pulled his cap down over his ears. "I ought to break his butt is what I ought to do. I'm telling you, I don't like it."

"He cares a lot about what you think, Amos, and I'm worried that he'll run off if he thinks that you're angry with him. At least pretend to keep an open mind so that we can find out where this Koch fellow is."

"Fine, Tomas." Amos said quietly. "Whatever."

"We're almost there." He placed a friendly hand on Amos'

shoulder. "Let's discuss it later."

Predatory lending.

Tomas stared thoughtfully at the man who sat across from

him and then eyed Amos who calmly chewed on the end of a cigar

while Tomas turned the two words about in his brain.

"Lending" he understood; "predatory" he understood.

Essentially, he was being called a predator who lent money. Yes,

Tomas nodded to himself. That sounded about right.

Benyamin Reuven, a big behemoth of a man – almost seven

feet tall, hairy and wiry, with a loud, nasally voice and a deeply

wrinkled forehead that sat above raccoon eyes that were set too

close together. It was Tomas' habit to look a man in the eye, but he

found that when he looked at Benyamin for too long his own eyes

would cross. He had made the trip especially for Benyamin – had

known he would have to make the trip when he loaned Benyamin

money weeks before.

The large man almost looked comical sitting in a small,

ragged armchair that was too small for his body. His big, bare feet stuck out awkwardly on either side of him and Tomas marveled at the spectacular size of the man's furry, great toe.

"So where is it?" Tomas asked.

"Where is what?"

"Come on, Ben. If you don't have the whole amount then of course I'm reasonable. I'll settle for the interest for now."

"You're not gonna shake me down." Benyamin jabbed a long index finger into his chest. "I know all about you, you rotten scoundrel. I'm not giving you anything."

Tomas stood and removed his jacket and glanced around the sparsely furnished, immaculate room as he calmly rolled his sleeves up. Besides the armchair that the giant sat atop, a clean mattress lay directly in the middle of the floor next to a makeshift table that held a small lamp with no bulb. Despite the cleanliness of the room, it carried an almost overwhelming odor of musty sweat.

"Looks like no one wants to live with you, Benyamin."

Benyamin's eyes shifted to rest on Joseph and John, but he did not speak.

"The Kaplan man, right?" Tomas asked with narrowed eyes.

"Maybe." Benyamin shrugged.

"Maybe. Yeah, that's why." Tomas stared steadily at Benyamin. "I was so pissed when he sent you down to me. You didn't think I knew, but I did. But then he's too much of a chicken shit to deal with me himself."

"Is that right?" Benyamin sat forward in his seat and rested his elbows on his knees and his eyes fell hesitantly upon Amos and the twins who stood leaning against the wall near the door.

"They won't bother you, Benyamin. You're dealing with me right now."

Still unsure, Benyamin turned and looked Tomas up and down in a way which indicated that he was not impressed.

"You see, that's why I gave you the loan, Benyamin, so that you could go back and tell Kaplan something that he doesn't know."

"What's that?" Benyamin suddenly stood to his full height and walked towards him.

"That I'll crack your fucking head just like I did his."

Benyamin did not see the knife as he swung his huge fist, but Tomas made sure he felt it, and as he ducked he brought the long, slim blade up and drove it between Benyamin's ribs then pulled it out and plunged it in again, relishing the feel of the sharp blade entering the man's flesh as smooth as slicing fresh bread, and he twisted the knife then and was satisfied with the yell of pain that bounced off the walls of the room.

Tomas swiftly moved around the back of Benyamin, ducking the man's flailing arms, and kicked him hard in the back of one knee. When Benyamin hit the floor, he rose on his hands and knees and attempted to crawl away, leaving large drops of blood in a trail behind him. Tomas kicked him over and Benyamin grunted, pressing a bloody hand to his side and tried to pull himself to his feet, but Tomas drove the sole of his boot into Benyamin's groin and the man yelped and grunted in agony as he hit the floor clutching his crotch.

Tomas stooped beside him then and wiped his blade on the shoulder of Benyamin's shirt.

"Where is it?" Tomas whispered.

"Go to hell!" Benyamin screamed then spat at him and Tomas grimaced in disgust when droplets from a warm spray of spittle landed on his cheek and mouth.

"Fucking spit!" Tomas exclaimed in repulsion.

Anger bubbled up inside of him until he thought he would burst. When he breathed, he could smell the stink of Benyamin's saliva up his nose and on his face, and Benyamin knew the effect that it was having on him because he laughed hysterically while Tomas pulled a handkerchief from his pocket and wiped his face with nausea-filled eyes.

"Joseph, where are the matches?"

Tomas' eyes never left Benyamin as Joseph headed towards him and placed a book of matches in his hand. The smirk left Benyamin's face and his eyes widened when Amos and John approached him and he tried again to stumble to his feet but he was too slow, and they were upon him before he could rise from the floor, and as the three men subdued him, Benyamin watched

with anxious eyes as Tomas deliberately leaned in front of him so

that he could watch the flame of a match burn out.

"Do you know what I'm doing?" Tomas asked as he held

the match in front of him.

And Benyamin did not answer but his eyes rested

questioningly on his face.

"The first eye, Benyamin, will be for the spit." Tomas said

this through clenched teeth. "There's no way around that." He

shook the match until the fire burned out then slung the stick over

his shoulder in agitation, the thought of Benyamin's wet saliva on

his own lips still repulsive. "But the second eye will go if you don't

pay me what you owe."

Tomas watched as the meaning of his words settled over

Benyamin, and he waited as the realization of what was about to

happen sunk into the man's brain, and before his struggles began

anew, Amos straddled his chest, being careful to tuck Benyamin's

arms beneath his own legs while the twins jumped upon his legs

and abdomen, restraining him to the floor. He began to scream then and Tomas laughed knowing that no one would come to his aid.

Unable to do much else, Benyamin's head thrashed frantically from side to side in an attempt to keep the flame away from his face, and Tomas kneeled over him and trapped Benyamin's head between his knees while Amos pried one of his eyes open. Tomas stared down at Benyamin, pleased to see that terror had found a place to settle in his brain and he lit a match and smiled as he brought the flame to rest on the white of one of Benyamin's exposed eyes.

As the fire sizzled out on his eyeball, a painful roar escaped Benyamin's throat and his body jerked off the floor in anguished spasms, but Amos rode him like a bull, pulling himself up higher onto the man's chest until his knees wrapped themselves around Benyamin's chin and the man writhed in pain beneath him, unable to escape the weight of three men lying across his body.

Amos shook his head when John laughed. "He's all burnt now."

Tomas lit another match and as the flame sparked,

Benyamin began to wail and tremble.

"Where?" Tomas asked with a lifted brow.

Though he cried, Benyamin sneered up at him and stubbornly shook his head, so Tomas threw the matchstick to the side and lit another, moving purposefully toward him as Amos straddled his chest, oblivious to the man's heavy panting, and Benyamin screamed when Amos suddenly grabbed his large head between strong fingers and pressed a thumb into his blistering eye.

"Wait! Wait!" He screamed.

Behind him, Tomas could hear the twins snickering together. "See, he's all gentle now, Tomas." John said soothingly.

"I have something better than money." Benyamin said through a pained breath. His breathing was erratic and sweat from pain and fear drenched his face and rolled into his ears in fat drops.

"Your eye is burning real bad, ain't it?" Amos asked in a curious voice and inspected Benyamin's face.

Benyamin did not respond but turned one good eye on him.

"Feels like it's on fire." Amos whispered then and stared

down at him with a cold, vacant stare. "If you lie, he's gonna burn your eyeballs outta your head. I know it. I done seen him do it."

"I'm bleeding to death." Benyamin said through clenched teeth.

Amos patted Benyamin on the face then got up off the man and gestured for Joseph and John to do the same. Painfully yet pitifully, Benyamin rolled into a sitting position and leaned against the wall. They waited as he checked his wound then pressed a hand to his bloody side and rested his head against the wall. His now disfigured face was stark white, wet and chalky in appearance, and he trembled so hard that his teeth chattered.

"Go on then." Amos encouraged softly.

Benyamin winced as he licked his dry lips. "There's a spy running with you."

"Aw, shut your lying trap." Joseph snarled then kicked at him.

Benyamin winced and stiffened as a new wave of pain hit him. He held a hand up to ward off further assault. "The girl that disappeared – what was her name?"

Tomas' heart began to pound as he waited for Benyamin's recall, but he was disappointed when the wrong name passed Benyamin's chapped lips.

"Ania." He whispered.

Amos staggered back a step but did not lose his composure. Ania, his love, had vanished months before without a trace just like Avigail. And she had not been deported to the camps just like Avigail.

Benyamin paused and fought to catch his breath. "He lies to them. Says he can get them out, but he robs them and turns them in. She knew. She was coming to tell you."

"Who?" Amos asked with wild eyes.

"I'm gonna bleed to death." Benyamin screamed.

Amos walked quickly over to him and pressed his boot against Benyamin's injured side and the man screamed and ranted obscenities at him until he relented.

"Who?" Amos asked again.

He could see the violent anger that surged through the twins and Benyamin knew by the ferocious look on Amos' face that *if he didn't talk the matches were coming back out.*

Tomas had been poised and ready to hear the one name that he hated, and he closed his eyes in anticipation, because ever since the day they had met, Tomas had fantasized about ripping Franco's conniving heart out and feeding it to him, but his eyes flew open in surprise and Amos exhaled painfully when the name escaped Benyamin's lips...

"Major."

"Slow down, Joseph." John called out to his brother as the four men made their way out of Benyamin's building.

"Do you realize how much he's overheard?" Joseph said in disbelief. "He knows everything."

Shocked into silence, Amos trailed behind them all with a dazed expression on his face.

"Let's talk to him first. We can't just turn on him because of what Benyamin says alone." Though John made an attempt toward optimism, his voice held the doubt that they all felt. "We'll just find out what he's about first, okay?"

Annoyed, Joseph shook his head and stuffed his hands into his pockets. They all worried as they walked and Tomas made a mental checklist of all the things that he knew that Major knew, and his mind traveled to Gideon and Jakob sitting alone waiting for him, and when he looked over to Amos, he could see mischievous thoughts playing across his face.

Tomas envied Amos that at least he had some lead as to what had happened to Ania. Avigail had gone missing before they had even encountered Major, so unless she had somehow made it to this Koch fellow on her own, he still had no lead as to what had happened to her. She had nothing when she left but the clothes on her back... and possibly a baby growing inside of her. He was determined to get down to the bottom of what was going on.

It had taken a bit of conjoling and old-fashioned ass kissing, but Tomas finally convinced Amos not to say anything to Major until they met with Wise Koch. If he hadn't been so on guard, he would have laughed out loud as he thought about the conversation that he had had with his uncle and father before he'd left to meet Amos and Major. He wondered now why he hadn't kept his thoughts to himself until he knew for sure, but their advice was invaluable, so he risked chastisement and intentionally waited until the last moment to tell them where he was going, and as he had known, they had agreed with Amos.

His father had stood in the middle of the floor wearing long thermal underwear with a dingy blanket wrapped around his shoulders. The expression on his face could only be described as stupefied and his mouth hung open in disbelief. In the months since Miriam had died, Gideon had lost a considerable amount of weight and nearly resembled the starving forms that huddled in the streets below. His hair had grayed considerably and now was more salt than pepper. Deep wrinkles had settled into the corners of his eyes and around his mouth, but his gaze had remained steady and sure.

"Nip it in the bud now, Tomas. If you go beyond that gate, you'll be shot."

"I have to know if he knows anything about Avigail."

"Have you lost your mind?" Gideon asked. He searched Tomas' face for sign of sickness and waited for a response.

"He's crazy like his mother."

They both turned and looked behind them at a grumpy Jakob. Under a shock of white, unkempt hair, his face held a glower full of bitter misery and wrinkles born of affliction, but his deep lines were not made from the grief of mourning alone, but from the kind of rage that one suffers when they have been wronged but have been denied vengeance – rage that has no quench, and Jakob's was akin to an inferno that had settled into his stomach and burned ferociously day and night.

"Avigail wouldn't step foot near a German." Gideon snapped. "And why would you go to the very house where you're probably being set up to be robbed?"

"And what of Major, Dad?"

"You'll get caught." Gideon pleaded.

"The Gestapo or a German! Oh boy. Choices, choices." Jakob said bitterly and then sarcastically rubbed his hands together in mock excitement and turned his mouth up.

"I'm just going to check it out." Tomas looked back and forth between them.

Gideon shook his head. *"I don't trust it."*

"If Major is involved then you're both in danger as well. He knows what I'm hiding here. I just want to check it out."

Gideon turned and walked over to Jakob and sat down beside him. The blanket fell from his shoulders as he pulled his boots on. *"I'm going with you."*

"No. I can move quicker if I don't have to worry about you. I'll be back before you know it."

"I don't like this, Tomas." Gideon repeated.

"If Major is a spy then he can hurt our chances of making it out alive. We're getting out of here, Dad. We can't just keep waiting around here like we're still in shock."

That got his uncle's attention and Jakob nodded his head in agreement.

Gideon slumped forward with his head in his hands and exhaled heavily. *"I don't want you to walk into a trap, son. I don't want to lose you."* Gideon's voice broke and he went silent.

Jakob stood and patted his nephew on the back. *"You're a good boy, Tomas. We will wait for you here. Come back to us with what you find and we will decide together."*

Major had not lied about the stench. As they passed the broken doors of apartments, terrified eyes stared out at them under the glow of dim candle light that illuminated their haggard faces and gave them the appearance of ghosts. Tomas did not let his eyes linger as he passed, but from what he could see, these ghosts' living conditions were beyond atrocious. Dirty dishes and pots lay piled upon one another and the foul odor of sewerage permeated the air.

Major led them to the end of the hall and down into the lower floor of the building. Amos removed his hat and placed it over his nose as they descended into the darkness and they stopped while Major pulled matches from his pocket to light the small lantern that he carried. As the room illuminated, Tomas' stomach turned as they made their way through piles of filthy rags and soiled, moldy mattresses.

"It's here." Major whispered.

He carefully stepped over a mess then lifted the light to

illuminate the wall before them and sure enough there was a hole large enough for him to crawl into and he passed the lamp to Amos then crawled inside. They waited as he scrambled around inside with just the heels of his worn boots showing then scooted backwards and came out of the hole with a small, green canvas bag.

"Okay. Got it." He said, brushing the dust from his clothes and then slung the bag over his shoulder.

When he went to retrieve the lamp from Amos, Amos would not release it, and held it there with both of them grasping it and Major did not lift his eyes to meet Amos', but calmly waited until he relinquished the lamp, and Amos stared suspiciously at Major's small back as he led them from the building.

As they made their way down Dzielna St. toward the cemetery, they moved with an alert, quiet stealth - and they had to move fast to keep up with Major. As they made their way through the tombstones, lights flashed about among the stones and they ducked to avoid them. They had expected patrols to be about and they held their breath as the lights slowly disappeared into the distance.

"Follow me." Major whispered.

As they made their way carefully through the streets, sometimes stopping to hide as automobiles passed or people moved in the streets, Amos and Tomas made the realization then that the air was fresher – cleaner. Life outside the ghetto seemed to be going on uninterrupted and seemingly oblivious to the horrors that were occurring just beyond the brick wall, and resentment flowed through Tomas and he was more convinced than ever that the time to escape was now.

It took them an hour to make it to their destination and as they came upon the dark farmhouse, Tomas could feel Amos tense beside him and he reached out and laid a reassuring hand upon his friend's shoulder. They avoided the front door and followed Major around to the back of the large house and then waited as he tapped at a side window.

"Who's there?" Came a quiet whisper from above them and Tomas jumped, startled, and looked up to search the house with his eyes but saw no one.

"It is Major."

"Come then."

They followed Major to the front of the dark house having
to keep up with his pace as he stooped and ran steadily to the now
open front door where a tall, blonde man awaited them. He
allowed them all to enter, but his eyes rested warily upon Tomas
and then a skeptical looking Amos.

"I didn't know you were bringing anyone, Major."

Tomas felt Amos cringe beside him at the sound of the
man's accent.

*"These are my friends from the Quarter. Remember I told
you about them?"* Major looked back and forth between the three
of them with a broad smile upon his face then held up the canvas
bag. *"I have the money and all my things like you said."*

Tomas wondered if Amos noticed Wise wince when Major
mentioned money.

"Where's Olivia?" Major asked excitedly.

"She's in the shed, Major."

Wise spoke to Major but his eyes remained upon an openly

hostile Amos. Even after Major departed, the three men still stood by the door and quizzically regarded one another, but Amos scowled openly and did not try to hide his distrust.

What caught Tomas' attention was the man's hands. They appeared soft like a woman's and he continually rubbed them across the front of his pants as if wiping some unseen substance onto his slacks and Tomas wondered if his hands were sweating.

"Please. We haven't met. I am Tomas and this is Amos." He stepped forward and extended a hand and Wise stared at it for a few moments before he took it, and Tomas realized that he was right – Wise's palm was sweaty and his hand was extremely soft. Tomas inwardly cringed and loosened his firm grip but smiled amicably in an attempt to seem friendly. Though the man had been caught off guard, Tomas still did not trust him.

"Please come in and have a seat."

Wise gestured for them to follow him into the kitchen and Tomas studied the back of the man the same as he had the front. He was plain looking, of average height, and slim with whitish-blonde hair and gray eyes.

"Into the kitchen? Really?" Amos said this almost too sarcastically and Tomas clenched his teeth and restrained the urge to cuff him.

Wise stopped in the middle of the floor with his back ramrod straight and turned and smiled. "Well, I was going to offer you coffee and the coffee is in the kitchen."

"You seem nervous." Amos said in a business-like, matter-of-fact tone.

Wise's eyebrows rose and Tomas saw that he was slightly amused by Amos' frankness. "I assure you that I am very nervous. I did not know that you were coming and I know that I don't have to tell you how very dangerous this is."

"Well, of course not. No one knows that better than me." Amos patted his chest but kept his openly distrustful eyes leveled upon Wise.

"I know that you do not trust me." Wise said calmly, as if he were speaking to a child. "And I understand why, but I am here to help you. That is all."

"Help me? But I thought you were here for the money?"

"I care about the plight of the Jews." Wise said as if offended.

"Then why charge them for safety?"

"I have to pay for supplies – candles, food. Not to mention the risk to my own life."

"Pssh." Amos dismissed Wise's words with a wave of his hand.

Wise's eyes narrowed at Amos' obvious expression of disdain. "Do you know the penalty for hiding a Jew?" He asked with a scorn filled tone.

"Do you?" Amos took a step toward him and jabbed a finger into his chest.

"Of course, I do. I –"

A door slammed shut behind them and they turned towards the kitchen where Major entered pulling a robust, dark-haired woman behind him. Her chubby cheeks were rosy from the outside chill and she held the collar of her sweater tightly about her neck. Seeing the pair standing awkwardly, Amos sauntered past Wise and into the kitchen as if it was his own house and pulled a chair from the table while rolling up his sleeves.

The woman watched him as he went because his eyes never left her from the time he entered the kitchen until he took his seat. Tomas followed Wise and they both entered the kitchen to watch the exchange. The warm room held the distinct aroma of baked sweets and on the long, scrubbed wooden table sat a plate of fresh blueberry muffins and when Tomas' stomach growled, Olivia looked over and gave him a kind, knowing smile. Tomas wondered about the woman. To him, she seemed harmless and her smile was friendly as she held onto Major's hand.

"You must be Olivia." Amos sat forward in his seat and placed his hands on his knees.

Seemingly cautious, but calm, Olivia returned Amos' glare with unwavering eyes. "I am Olivia. Amos, right? And you must be Tomas." She looked over to Tomas and nodded before her eyes returned to Amos.

"Where are you from, Olivia?"

"My family is from Lodz."

"Lodz?" Amos sat back in his seat and folded his arms.

"And how long have you been here with Koch?"

"A month, maybe a little more." Confused, she turned to Wise and then to Tomas.

Amos raised his eyebrows in surprise. "Why so long?"

With a smirk, Wise folded his arms across his chest and stared at Amos with obvious dislike.

"I was sick for a while when I arrived and then as the others came I stayed longer to help Wise." She answered.

"How very brave of you. And you just wander around outside without fear, eh?" Amos stared at her for long moments and the tension in the room became so thick that it was almost suffocating.

Tomas noticed the involuntary twitching of Wise's hands as he watched the conversation transpire between the pair. He then wiped his hands down the front of his trousers and brought them back to his side to fidget with the material of his pants leg, rolling it between his fingers only to slide his hands down the front of his trousers again.

"But you will be leaving soon?" Amos asked with his head

cocked to one side.

"Why are you badgering this woman?" Wise exclaimed.
"Olivia, please put on the coffee."

Amos swiftly turned in his seat and glared at Wise with
such dark contempt that the man jumped, and for a moment,
Tomas thought that Amos was going to strike him, as did everyone
else in the room from the look on their faces, and Tomas pushed
himself from the wall and prepared to intervene. He knew that
Amos wanted to snap at the least provocation from the man, but
Tomas still wanted information from him. Luckily, Amos turned
and changed course.

"Major, I have something to ask you. Come here and sit
down please."

Amos' voice was tense as he pulled a chair towards him
and patted the seat, motioning for Major to sit down. When the boy
was seated, Amos pulled his chair towards him until they sat eye-
to-eye and then he reached out and pulled Major's cap from his
head and ruffled his hair.

"Major." He whispered.

Tomas momentarily closed his eyes and hoped that the boy was as innocent as he seemed. Major, on his part, had lost his jolly expression. The vibes that the adults were giving off were not good, and Wise, although seemingly cool, had begun to sweat and his face shone in the bright light of the kitchen.

"Yes, Amos." Major muttered, fumbling with an ear with the three remaining fingers of his right hand.

"Who else do you know that has left through this underground?"

Major held his good hand up and counted off the names. "There was Jojo and his mother, Mr. Issacs who was here with them and –"

Wise cleared his throat and Major paused and stared up at him in confusion, but when Amos turned on Wise with a snarl, he held his hands up defensively and took a step back.

Amos' irritated gaze fell back to Major. "How did you meet him?"

"He helped me and Jojo sometimes. Gave us water."

"And I told them that if they knew of anyone that needed

help that they could come to me. I have always been good to you, Major, haven't I?" Wise asked in an exasperated tone.

"Yes." Major said then turned back to Amos.

"Tell me, Koch, what exactly is this underground?" Amos asked and got up from his seat then slid his chair beneath the table. He slowly approached Olivia, all the while looking her from head to toe, but she did not flinch and stared him directly in the eye.

Wise's voice seemed suddenly tired. "It is what it sounds like. Once passage is paid, arrangements are made to move individuals from one place to another and eventually across the border where they are able to start a new life."

"And for how long have you been so gracious to offer this help?"

Wise stared at Amos with pity. "A year almost."

A low whistle escaped Amos' lips. "And how much do you charge these 'individuals' for your help?"

"Whatever they can afford. Some can afford more than others."

"Then that means you'll take any poor sap that comes in, in need of assistance."

Wise chuckled and looked at Amos as if he were dull in the head. "Well, within reason of course."

"Of course." He turned to Olivia then. "And how much have you paid?"

"I mean – well, I..."

Caught off guard, Olivia sputtered then went silent and looked to Wise for assistance and Amos' eyes narrowed dangerously. "From Lodz, did you say?"

"I did."

The fine hairs on the back of Tomas' neck stood up while Amos glowered at the woman. He strained his ears to hear his friend's low whisper. "Tell me why you are here."

"You know why I am here." Olivia looked bewildered and backed away from him.

"You are good, but not that good. And if you are a Jew than I am a toad." Amos turned and pointed at Tomas. "And he is a giraffe."

Tomas was relieved to hear the surprised inhalation of breath from Major and the boy looked back and forth between the two in surprised confusion.

"You are mad." Olivia exclaimed.

Amos turned from the woman and went to kneel in front of Major. The look in his eyes was pained and he opened his mouth then closed it and stared at Major then smiled. "You know, I never had a little brother. Always wanted one but..." Amos shrugged his shoulders.

"What is it, Amos?" Major asked with tears shining in his eyes.

Amos grabbed Major's face between his hands and the boy let out a startled gasp. "Tell me, Major, did you bring Ania here?"

"I did."

Tomas' reaction was too slow as Amos moved swiftly toward Wise, and before he knew it, Amos had grabbed Koch and slammed him into the wall.

"Tell me where she is." He growled into his face. "Or I'm going to hurt you."

Major jumped from his seat. "Let him down, Amos! She left on the underground. Mr. Koch helped her get away. She didn't want you to know that she was going."

"Who told you that?" Tomas asked with surprise and Major turned and pointed, but Olivia was already gone from the room.

"Where?" Amos growled menacingly into Koch's face.

"She's gone – probably across the border by now." Koch stuttered.

As Amos slammed Koch to the floor and pummeled him, Tomas moved frantically about the kitchen and pantry searching for where Olivia may have disappeared to and he cursed himself for allowing her to take advantage of the commotion and slip away.

"She left her things – her money. She loved me. She wouldn't have left without saying so." Amos turned to Major and yelled angrily. "How could you keep that from me?"

Major had begun to cry and fat tears escaped his eyes and rolled down his cheeks. "Olivia said..." He stopped then and collapsed on the floor in grief. "I'm sorry, Amos. Ania told me to bring her here. She was talking to Olivia and when I came back she was already gone."

The loud crack of gunfire startled them all and Amos dove across the room towards Major and pulled him flat to the floor. Tomas moved quickly across the room and shut off the lamp, and they crawled quickly to the back door and pulled it open just as a bullet struck the wood above their heads. Up on their feet and outside, they ran from the kitchen as fast as they could go and into the darkness beyond the house. They could hear the voices of Wise and Olivia behind them and then two more cracks split the air and they ducked but kept moving. Then three more cracks and Major collapsed to the ground, taking Amos with him. Tomas turned and went back for them and yanked Major up by his coat, but the boy was dead weight in his arms and he fell to his knees and pulled the boy to him and shook him.

"Major." He shook him violently then smacked him across the face. "Major, get up."

Wild-eyed, Amos stared around them, peering into the

darkness for Koch and Olivia, and avoided looking down at Major's small, motionless body. Tomas rested his hand at the back of the boy's head and it was quickly filled with warm, oozing liquid and he cursed harshly. Another two cracks cut the air and they jumped to attention at the sounds of screeching tires crunching gravel and barking dogs filling the air. Tomas gently laid Major upon the ground and he and Amos raced off into the night.

They could hear the thick, guttural accents and heavy boots hitting the ground all around them as they went and they were soon surrounded. The dogs got to them before the SS did, and Tomas and Amos fought to keep them from sinking long canines into their throats as they were attacked. Tomas pulled his blade from his pocket and stabbed at the dog that held his arm between jaws that felt like shredding vice grips and he was relieved to hear the hairy beast yelp before it released him.

Laughter rang out all around them as they fought with the vicious beasts and by the time the lights of the Humvees showed upon them, they had grown exhausted and the dogs began to get the best of them. Tomas fought as hard as he could, faltering *slightly as they laughed and purposely blinded him with their flashlights, but his blade sent another dog to the ground twitching and yelping in pain and he started on another who had several seconds before sunk sharp teeth into the muscular flesh of his calf.*

He could hear Amos beside him cursing bitterly as SS men rushed at him with their feet and Tomas knew that his friend fought for all he was worth. As he brought his blade up and into the ribcage of the growling beast at his leg, they finally pulled the dogs off and instead of jumping to his feet, Tomas felt along the ground for Amos and sighed with relief when he heard him laughing hysterically in front of him.

"Get up!" Rough hands grabbed him by the back of his collar and Tomas was yanked to his feet.

He winced as his weight bore down on his injured leg, but he didn't cry out, and instead tried to make count of the men around him. A bright light shone in his face and he staggered backwards and attempted to shield his eyes with a bloody forearm. When his eyes focused, he could make out the face of a tall, dark-haired man standing in front of him in Nazi attire, his long leather coat flapping in the wind, and four more SS men surrounded he and Amos who lay on the ground on his back bloody and heaving heavily. His face had begun to purple and swell and he stared at Tomas out of one unbloodied eye and they understood one another.

Tomas turned back to the officer who stood before him and he did not waver or lower his eyes at the direct hatred that flowed from the man – he wanted him to know that the feeling was mutual.

"Grab my boots and beg me and maybe I will let you go back to the ghetto." The SS man said this with a sneer and pointed a finger at the ground.

Tomas followed that finger with his eyes then looked up at the man and did as Amos would have done and spit on the ground between them. The officer's thick mustache twitched and he lifted his gloved fist and backhanded Tomas across the face.

Tomas looked over to Amos who winked, signaling that he was willing to die for his dignity, so Tomas turned back to the officer and hissed...

"I am not a woman."

And he relished the surprised look from the officer as he

swung the fist attached to his good arm and smashed it as hard as he could into the man's face, and as he heard the crunch of bone and as warm blood spurted onto his fist he was immensely satisfied at the pitiful scream that escaped the man as he clutched his hands to his bleeding face then fell to the ground.

Tomas found himself fighting unconsciousness then and pain ricocheted up into his head and warm blood ran down his face and into his eyes, blinding him. The second strike of a heavy object upon the base of his skull depleted his strength and Tomas collapsed onto the ground while men swarmed around him cursing hatefully. As blow upon blow fell upon him and darkness overtook him, he could hear Amos' defiant laughter slowly fading away, and as he drifted into darkness, his heart burst as he thought about Jakob and Gideon awaiting his arrival back to the Quarter, and then his father's sure grief when he realized that his son would never return.

He was there taunting him again. He did not know how long it had been. He had drifted in and out of consciousness and *the bite wound on his leg burned. His mouth was dry and he tried to lick his chapped lips so that he could respond to the mocking going on above him. He grunted then and tried to force his voice to work if only for this last time and he succeeded in prying his tongue loose from where it clung to the roof of his mouth.*

Shit. He smelled shit. He was standing in it, soft and mushy under his feet. He shifted his weight to his good leg and placed his hands on the walls around him. He was dizzy and wanted to sit down but there was no room. It was dark and cold and the only dim light came from what he thought was a hole somewhere above his head. Tomas forced himself to concentrate on the voice above him.

"Jew dog. Did you shit yourself?"

Tomas took a deep breath and fought another wave of dizziness. "I know who you are." He said with a choked, hoarse voice. "Let me out of here and I'll break your face again."

Cruel laughter met his ears and Tomas screamed and growled with rage. "You hit like a bitch... burn your fucking eyes out of their sockets... thieving son of a bitch... twist your head off your neck with my bare hands. You weak fuck, you had better kill

me."

Then Tomas was left alone in the small cell and he thought

of Gideon – almost alone. Suddenly an all-consuming fury drove

him insane and he went mad, screaming and ranting, irate that he

was standing in filth, enraged that he was being held prisoner by

men that he thought to be inferior to himself, and a violent storm

brewed in that cramped confinement. Breathing like a bull,

muscles taut and pulsating, veins bulging in the sides of his neck,

he beat at the walls and himself, spending his wrath until his

knuckles bled and the cell felt as if it were closing in on him.

CHAPTER TWO

Oak Park, 1958

Scarlett fed Amir and watched her husband from the corner of her eye. He was agitated tonight, the same as he had been for several weeks now, and he stared blankly at the table in front of him and absentmindedly chewed his dinner. He swallowed mechanically, and to her surprise, tilted his head upward as if listening for something and his hard, hazel eyes dimmed and he laid his fork on his plate then slumped back in his seat. Scarlett turned and studied him then – the deep frown that creased his brow and the dark intensity of his eyes.

"The nightmares have started again?"

Tomas settled his gaze on her and raised his eyebrows in acknowledgement of her question but did not reply. She was relieved that Amir was quiet. His mood had been mild all day and she examined him then – his dark hair and lively, brown eyes. Her perfect little boy.

She wiped applesauce from his face with a napkin then picked him up from his high chair and sat him on his feet and he took off on short, chubby legs to the living room to play with his toys.

"Tomas?"

"I don't want to talk about this, Scarlett."

"Why not, Tomas? I am your wife."

"Lower your voice. The boy is in the next room."

Scarlett whispered through clenched teeth. "I am your wife."

"And I am telling you that I don't want to talk about it. Leave it be."

"That is not fair. I am the one that has to live with you – sleep with you."

Tomas looked around her toward Amir then pointed a finger at her in warning. "You know what's wrong, Scarlett, but you always want to dredge it all up. I said let it be."

"You're hiding something."

Tomas sat back in his seat and sighed. He enfolded his hands behind his head and waited for her.

"You're staying away from home again." Scarlett wagged

a finger at him. "If I didn't know any better, I would think that there was another woman."

"No, my love. I'm not done with you yet."

"This is not a joke, Tomas."

Amused, he smiled and winked at her. "Come here, Scarlett."

"Don't try to change the subject."

"But I want you, sweetheart."

"No, Tomas. I'm upset with you. If the tables were turned, you wouldn't let me get away with what you're doing to me right now."

"You are mine. I am supposed to know you like the back of my hand." He held up a large, calloused hand – a hand that she adored.

Scarlett shifted her weight from one foot to the other and placed her hands on her hips. "Are you not mine as well?"

He chuckled then and her heart skipped a beat at the way his eyes caressed her. "Yes, we are married, but it is different. You are a woman. You belong to me."

Scarlett rolled her eyes skyward and Tomas snorted with laughter.

"I am not property, Tomas."

"But I have papers that say you belong to me."

"And I have the very same papers."

Tomas admired his wife from where she stood. Her hair was long now and dark curls hung to her small waist in thick, silken ringlets. She was biting on a knuckle as she had a habit of doing when she concentrated, and he felt the familiar flame begin to lick at his loins and he hardened as he watched the ball of a finger disappear into her mouth, and then he groaned as her soft lips enclosed it and drew it into the warm wetness there, and he reached down and adjusted his pants as her pink tongue darted around the side of it then lazily moved about.

"I take care of you. I feed you, clothe you. Your body is mine to take when I please." He whispered.

Scarlett looked up then and as his dark eyes bore into her own, her nipples tightened beneath her blouse and a moist, sensual throbbing started in her own loins, but she ignored her body and

Tomas' seductive eyes and began to clear dishes from the table, being careful not to stray too close to him.

"And that is why you won't let me work." She said quietly.

Tomas' eyes were the ones to roll skyward this time and he exhaled an aroused breath. "Not now, Scarlett."

"I want to work, Tomas."

He rubbed an agitated hand over his brow and motioned to her with his hand. "Come here, Scarlett."

"I can find someone to care for Amir during the day."

"You have your hands full here." Tomas' tone of voice told her that the conversation was over and she frowned with disappointment. "Come here, sweetheart, and sit on my lap."

"Do it yourself." She snapped before turning and stumping into the kitchen.

***

She nervously pulled at the hem of her skirt, her eyes intent upon him as he left the restaurant. Though she couldn't see his face, she knew him by the way that he walked – stiff-backed and wide-legged with his head lowered as if he owned the sidewalk. He was with another man and together they strolled to the corner and got into a silver pickup truck.

"You have to do this, Scarlett. You need to know who he is. I'll go with you if you want."

Those were the words that Michael had spoken to her that morning over the telephone. She hadn't wanted Michael's company. If Tomas was doing something terrible - as Michael so eagerly wanted her to believe - she did not want her friend there to witness it. He was her husband after all and when this was over, no matter what she found, she would be sure to ask Michael to mind her own damn business. She was not blind after all, and saw things with her own two eyes, of course – saw the way that people stepped off of the sidewalk and into the street to let Tomas pass. He had no friends. At least that she knew of. But he was not at all a friendly person to begin with.

She thought these things while she sat in the backseat of the taxi in utter apprehension and waited. She could see him sitting in the front seat of the truck conversing with the man that sat next to him, and Scarlett sat back in her seat and worriedly chewed her *fingernails. She had thought about turning back several times, but she didn't know when she would have another opportunity to get away again. Today she had done something that she had never done before and left Amir with a neighborhood girl so that she could find out what Tomas was about. Right now he expected her to be home with Amir preparing dinner, and if he saw her, he would think that she was spying on him – which she was. She had decided to risk his anger. She was that curious. She told herself that she deserved to know. She was his wife after all.*

Scarlett, she kept telling herself, when you share a bed with someone you have a right to know what secrets they are keeping.

And Tomas was definitely keeping secrets.

"What do you wanna do, lady?" The cab driver asked and stared back at her through the rearview mirror.

Scarlett worried the knuckle of her thumb with her teeth and sighed. "That's my husband. I just want to follow him. Okay?"

"It's your money, lady." Then, "He stepping out on you, eh?"

"I think so." Scarlett agreed, not knowing what else to say,

and unwilling to explain herself.

"Huh." Came the indifferent reply.

The silver truck began to move and as it pulled into traffic, Scarlett gave the driver a twenty dollar bill and nervously admonished him to be discreet while following the other vehicle.

***

Her heart pounded as the cab pulled to the corner and she watched Tomas disappear into a small, one-story brick building. The building was plain and had no sign on it, but two cars sat in the lot beside the silver pickup truck that Tomas had arrived in. She watched an old woman in a ragged coat push a cart down the street and she hesitated and wondered if she should just turn around and go home.

She could go home and get Amir – have a nice evening with her family and then let Tomas make love to her until she forgot…but then she would never know why he disappeared without explanation. After Amir was born, Tomas came home most nights – but he was gone throughout the day and Scarlett wanted badly to know what kept him so long away from her.

She clutched her purse to her abdomen and exited the cab

before she lost her nerve and ran back to the safety of her home.

Other than the old woman, no one else appeared on the empty

block and Scarlett squinted in the sunlight and peered at the

building before sprinting across the street.

She approached the metal door and exhaled a sigh of relief

when she pulled at the steel latch and found it locked. She looked

nervously about her and thought once again of fleeing to the safety

of her home...to the frustration of the unknown...

Scarlett ignored the pounding of her heart and ran down

the sidewalk and around to the back of the building. A tall, wire

gate surrounded the lush, green foliage in the rear of the building

and Scarlett flinched when the gate creaked as she pulled it open.

She could hear male voices coming from the dwelling and she

stopped dead in her tracks as Tomas' gruff baritone reached her

ears.

Petrified, but now unwilling to turn back, Scarlett eased

her wobbly knees along the building, looking around as she went,

and crept across the lawn until she stood below a large window

261

covered in thick, steel bars, and she held her breath and crouched

beside a large bush and listened to the voices coming from inside.

* * *

    Tomas chuckled to himself while he listened to the fat,

balding man that sat across from him. He looked about the muggy,

dimly lit office and wrinkled his nose at the funky odor that emitted

from the man. Felix was known for being a slovenly glutton, and

Tomas shook his head in revulsion at the greasy man and the dirty

t-shirt that he wore. Whenever Felix gestured, the fat around his

arms jiggled and he exposed dark sweat stains beneath his

armpits. Cigarette smoke swirled lazily in the air above his head

and he nervously ran a dark tongue over large, yellowed teeth.

    "What do you mean, you sold it?" Tomas asked, amused.

    Felix's hands shook as he ashed his cigarette in the stone

ashtray that sat amidst the clutter of his desk. He kept his eyes on

the gold watch that had settled between the sweaty folds of his

wrist and threatened to cut off circulation to his arm. He spoke

slowly, carefully, and as his jowls moved, Tomas' eyes rested on

the red rash that had settled into the creases of his flabby neck.

"Someone bought my debt." He shrugged and his breasts jiggled. "I sold it."

Tomas rolled his eyes, becoming impatient. "So where's my money, Felix?"

Felix's eye began to twitch and the man became so anxious that his voice squeaked. "It'll get paid. What I'm saying is that the money won't come from me."

"Let's recap." Tomas sat forward in his seat. "You wanted to bet on horses. I took your bet and you loss. Am I saying that right?"

Felix nodded but did not look up.

Tomas leaned back in his seat and allowed his chin to rest on his chest as he looked Felix over, enjoying the man's angst. "If you're trying to rob me, Felix, you'd better put some bass in your voice."

"I wouldn't – no, Tomas." The man said as if Tomas was confused. "Someone else was interested in taking it over. That's all I'm saying."

"Are you stupid, Felix?"

Felix looked up then into Tomas' eyes and sighed, thinking again of the white, cash filled envelope that rested quietly in the top drawer of his desk just inches from where he sat. He didn't want trouble from Tomas. Though fair, the man was relentless and overbearing, and Felix owed him money – a debt that he knew he was expected to pay with either money or grief. But he had been assured that Tomas would not bother him again, and so he leaned on earlier assurances and did as he had been told.

Under a hazel, predatory glare, Felix pulled a white card from his pants pocket and held it out to Tomas who stared at him as if he were crazy before reaching out with a swiftness that startled him, snatching the card from his hand.

Felix breathed a shaky sigh of relief when Tomas' eyes widened as he read the bold, black words that had been written on the stiff paper, and he sniffed with satisfied surprise when Tomas jumped from his seat and bolted from the room without a word or backward glance.

Scarlett's mind was on escape when Tomas came slamming

out of the back door and she ducked down then let out a curse when his back stiffened and he halted mid-step. She had expected him to leave the same way as he had arrived – through the front door – and she knew that he had seen her even before he turned. When he did face her, Scarlett shrank back in fear at the anger that burned from his eyes and into her own. There she stood – cowering halfway behind a bush looking guilty as sin and Tomas was shocked into outrageous speechlessness.

He pointed a finger to the ground in front of him and Scarlett felt like a whipped child. As she approached him, she wished that he had not been standing so close to the opening of the gate because she would have ran all the way home and locked him out of the house. Instead, as she made her way over to him, her eyes never left the ground, and she shrieked when he grabbed her roughly by the arm and yanked her alongside him and down the street. He did not speak, but Scarlett could feel the rage flowing from him and she shrank inside and nearly tripped over her feet in her haste to keep up with his long strides.

She had been staring at the ground for so long that she

didn't notice him hail a taxi, and so she was surprised when the yellow, checkered car pulled up alongside them. Tomas snatched the door open and nearly flung her inside before slamming the door closed. After giving instructions to the driver, he stepped back onto the curb, and Scarlett chanced a look at him as the car pulled away. His icy eyes bore directly into her own and she knew beyond a shadow of a doubt that she had trouble coming her way.

Once Tomas reached the neat, middle-class neighborhood Scarlett no longer resided in his thoughts. All he felt was apprehension mixed with frantic anticipation. Emotions that he hadn't felt in many years threatened to overwhelm him and his pace quickened as he searched the houses for the address on the card. When he finally found the home, he was stunned to see that it really existed and he stood on the sidewalk in front of it – took in the fresh, gray paint, the enclosed porch, the neatly trimmed lawn.

Slowly, he approached the door with his hands in his pockets and stood there at first without knocking and took deep breaths, trying to still his rapidly beating heart. But before he could raise a hand to knock, the front door was thrown open and

he peered through the screen door, through the dimness of the

enclosure at the tall, slim man who stood calmly in front of him

and studied him with the same rapt concentration.

A familiar, eerie feeling settled over Tomas then and he

ducked his head and inhaled a pained breath as an age old hand

reached out and grasped his heart in a death grip. He lifted a

shaky hand and pulled the screen door open and stepped inside but

with each step that he took, he felt as if he were retreating – being

pulled back in time.

Tomas approached the tall, still figure and prepared for a

hearty embrace. His arms lifted involuntarily seeking a familiar,

friendly hug, but the figure quickly retreated into the dimness of

the house, so he followed and stepped into a cluttered room – a

room where a clock sat on each of the four walls.

Tomas counted them. One gold, one brass, two black – all

ticking together until the sound became in one's ear almost

deafening. Another small alarm clock sat alone on a card table

next to a large armchair that faced a window where the only view was the side of the house next door, and Tomas did not wonder

what his friend saw when he peered out at the windowless brick.

But Tomas found that his hope and readiness for a happy

reunion was short lived, and as they stood and stared at one

another for several seconds without speaking, Amos' eyes shot

sparks of hatred at him and he was taken aback.

But as his eyes roamed over his old friend, he noticed that

life had truly taken its toll on Amos. His once thick, black hair was

now barely stubble on his head and his silver-gray eyes were

sharper. He glared at Tomas under thin, dark brows – his once

youthful skin now weathered and nearly stark white. Deep wrinkles

had settled into the creases that surrounded his eyes. He was still

tall and wiry, but hard muscle had settled in around his arms and

shoulders.

Though Tomas' heart had started instantly at the sight of

Amos and though he wanted to embrace him as a brother, he

remembered Amos, and he knew that if his friend was feeling

vengeful he would take Tomas' play for friendship as weakness, so

Tomas did not flinch, but made direct eye contact, as was his habit, and with obvious deliberation, took the three steps that closed the gap between them until they stood face to face.

"It is good to see you, Amos."

Amos looked Tomas from his head to his feet then up again. "Back up, Tomas."

"Come now, Amos –"

"Give me three feet." Amos said sternly, and held up three fingers.

Amused, Tomas held his hands out to his side and took a giant step backwards.

"I should kill you."

Now totally taken aback, Tomas staggered back another step in surprise at the ferocity of Amos' statement and the violent look in his eyes. Amos pointed a finger at him, seemingly fighting for control of his emotions.

"What is wrong with you?" Tomas asked, trying to keep the pain he felt from causing his voice to tremor.

"You're a traitor." Amos said through clenched teeth. He enfolded his hands in front of him, balling one hand into a fist and *grasping it tightly within the other while scowling at Tomas. His breathing came in short, hard pants.*

"Traitor?" Tomas shook his head and stared at the floor in confusion.

"Yeah. Traitor. And you know exactly what I'm talking about. I saw you leave that day with them. They walked you right out of the camp."

"So that makes me a traitor?" Tomas screamed in rage.

"They gave you a fucking blanket and everything, you sorry —"

"So you don't even ask me? You just accuse me, Amos?"

"I saw you. I saw the guilt in your face." Amos screamed back and pointed at his own steely, gray eyes.

"No, Amos. That was helplessness. That was grief."

"You're a liar." Amos spat and shook his head. "I saw you with my own eyes talking to the SS in that quaint little office while I knelt on rocks for hours! And then you lied when I asked you – you lied."

"You know me, Amos." Tomas said and placed his hand to

his chest. *"It's not what you think."*

"What about the food, Tomas?"

Tomas shook his head and tried to calm the thunder that rumbled in his ears.

Amos laughed and rubbed his stomach. "They fed you."

"I didn't take it."

"I saw you!" Amos spat.

"You saw me being offered. You never saw me take anything. Let me explain –"

"You should have explained then." Amos shook his head in outright disbelief.

"I couldn't trust you with that then, Amos."

"You're full of shit."

"Let me explain." Tomas begged.

"I did see you being walked out though, right? Or am I crazy there too?"

"You're wrong, Amos. You know me. You know I wouldn't –"

"I don't know you."

Amos took on the smug look of dislike that he had carried when they were boys, but it was now refined and unnerving in its quality. Tomas knew from experience with Amos that he should keep his eyes open.

As if he had read Tomas' mind, Amos smiled. "You have a wife now. A gentile. I saw her. She's beautiful. And a son – the savior of your life, Tomas, because I swear by this right hand," Amos held up a pale, calloused palm and pointed at it, "that if it were not for Amir, I would kill you."

The look of intended disrespect from Amos shook Tomas to his core and he laughed - awkwardly. He suddenly felt an urge to run and he felt silly - like a woman - so he pointed a finger at his old comrade, feeling the tension in his body as it cried out for him to flee.

Was he guilty?

His tongue clung to the roof of his mouth and his muscles clenched with dread as the distant memory of feeble, bent backs and pitiful bodies pressed against one another in the night begging for heat, shivering uncontrollably in the cold, weeping into the early morning from sorrow and sickness, made his budding anger dissipate and he shook his head with disappointment.

"You're a disgrace." Amos looked at Tomas as if he had crawled from beneath a rock.

"This isn't over, Amos." Tomas warned and willed his feet to move across the floor. When he made it to the door, he turned and looked back at Amos who turned his head and spit on the floor before turning back to him.

"Traitor."

Tomas left the house in a daze, and as he walked away he felt off balance. He was overwhelmed with confusion, with hurt, with rage. But he knew that he would return. After emotions settled and pain seared his soul to completion, his spirit would start to tingle just as a limb did when it had been asleep for too long.

When his heart was again revived, he would return to Amos and force him to listen to reason. He refused to lose his friend again.

***

Scarlett paced the sidewalk in front of the house and dared

not step foot on the porch. It was dark out and she knew that Tomas was inside because the lamp in the front hall was on. In her head she could see him inside now, sitting in the darkness of the living room in the wicker, straight backed chair that she had ordered from a magazine while she was still pregnant with Amir. She had thought herself to be modern then standing barefoot and big bellied in the kitchen with her fingers entwined in the tightly wound telephone cord while she spoke to the saleswoman.

She sighed nervously and chewed her bottom lip as guilt flowed through her. Tomas had been a good husband. She and Amir were well cared for and he indulged their every whim. He rarely raised his voice when speaking to her, even when upset…but then she knew how far she could take him. She knew when to let him be.

Scarlett also knew that when she opened the door he would be enraged. He expected her to be home with Amir, not outside in the dark pacing the lawn. She gravely studied the house and dreaded going inside, but she knew that the longer she remained absent, the more upset he would become.

Scarlett blew out a tense breath and forced her legs to move towards the porch. At the front door she paused and braced herself for an angry tirade then slipped her key into the lock and stepped inside. She stood there in the dimly lit hall and leaned against the door, catching her breath as her hand rested on the doorknob behind her. She was not prepared to stray too far from a means of escape.

The house felt still and silent, as if empty, but she knew he was there sitting in the dark beyond the dim glow of light that shone into the living room from the lamp. Scarlett tried to calm her breathing and momentarily her eyes closed and she waited for her thundering heart to calm as she tuned her ears to her surroundings.

When she heard him move, she quickly turned and pulled at the doorknob, not realizing that the lock had engaged. She pulled at the door, yanking desperately at the knob, but he was already there behind her and reached over her head to slam the door shut in her face and she rested her hands against the mahogany, feeling defeated, and did not turn when his chest rested heavily against her back.

She tried to gauge his mood without looking at him and the tenseness of his body mingled with the harsh breathing that fanned the nape of her neck told her that she would fare better if she didn't talk too much.

"Turn around."

Scarlett turned and faced him then gasped with surprise when he reached out and grasped her face in one large hand while three strong fingers made their way roughly into her mouth as he shoved her head into the door. Surprised, Scarlett tried to wrench free but he held her head in a vice grip with the palm of his hand roughly cupping her chin.

The scar near his lip twitched and he looked her over before bending and whispering in her face. "I should beat the hell out of you."

Scarlett turned her head and again tried to free herself then bit down on his fingers to no avail. He only gripped her jaw harder until she yelled out then waited patiently until she stopped squirming before removing his hand and releasing her.

She glared at him in disbelief. "I wouldn't have to follow you if you didn't keep secrets, Tomas."

Scarlett ducked as his palm slammed into the wood beside her head. He pointed a finger at her and spoke through clenched teeth and Scarlett cowered at the coldness in his eyes.

"Don't play on me, woman. You know damn well you shouldn't have been there. Right?"

Scarlett did not respond.

"Right!" Tomas screamed this and Scarlett flinched and blinked back tears.

"Tomas –"

"Shut up!"

Scarlett closed her mouth though she wanted to calm him and she again regretted her decision to follow him. Slowly she raised her hands and rested them lightly on his shoulders. When he didn't push her away, she moved in closer and stood on the tips of her toes to place a warm kiss at the base of his throat and he reached up and entwined his fingers in her hair.

"I'm so sorry, Tomas." He looked into her eyes and she

pleaded with him. "I will never do that again."

He suddenly yanked her from the door by her hair and roughly shoved her toward the stairs. "It's not going to be that easy, Scarlett."

She stumbled when he released her, but quickly regained her footing and fled. In a panic, she took the steps two at a time, frantically turning to look over her shoulder as she went, and though Tomas did not quicken his pace, the look in his eyes told her that he meant to put his hands on her.

Once she made it to their bedroom, she slammed the door behind her and reached up to engage the lock, but before she could place her fingers upon it, the door was flung open and Tomas crashed into the room like a raging bull.

"Tomas. Please, sweetheart." Scarlett held shaky hands out in front of her.

"I can't believe you followed me." Tomas raged in disbelief. "When I'm done with you, you're going to wish you stayed home with our son like a good wife."

His facial expression was filled with resentment and though

Scarlett knew that he felt betrayed, she still had to bite her tongue

lest a sharp retort pass between her lips and worsen her current

situation. His eyes moved threateningly over her and she recoiled

at the intended threat there.

"Tomas, don't hit me."

Tomas closed the door behind him and locked it without

ever taking his eyes from her face.

Scarlett tried to control the wobbling of her knees. "I

shouldn't have done it. I know. I won't ever do it again."

"I know you won't."

The finality of his tone and the coldness of his eyes as he

moved toward her frightened Scarlett more than his anger – he

was now too calm.

"Tomas, don't hit me."

He smiled then – a chilly tilting of his lips that did not

reach his eyes. "Where's my son?"

For the first time ever she wanted to lie to him – wanted to

tell him that Amir would be home at any moment, but the

aggression in him washed over her and she was intimidated.

"He's across the street." She whispered the truth.

Tears stung her eyes and she took a step backwards while he removed his shirt. His eyes had taken on a wicked, wolfish gleam. "Take your clothes off."

Caught off guard, Scarlett took another step back and watched him with suspicious eyes as he removed his belt. "Tomas."

When he came for her she tried to run but he was too quick and grabbed her roughly by the forearms and swung her body across the room. Scarlett went flying through the air only to land on the bed in a terrified heap. She soon realized that scurrying away was not an option when he grabbed her slim ankle in an iron grip and drug her towards him. Scarlett screamed and kicked at him to no avail and he stared her directly in the eyes as he grabbed her by the collar of her dress and ripped it clear down the center.

"Stop it, Tomas!" Scarlett screamed, but he grabbed her by her hair and twisted her body until she lay on her stomach.

He rested a knee in the small of her back then and ripped her dress to shreds then tore her underwear off, baring her naked flesh to his angry gaze. With his weight pressed firmly down upon her, Scarlett was unable to move and she screamed in frustration, and as the first stinging lash of the belt fell across her buttocks she inhaled a sharp, shocked breath then howled in pain.

She struggled with him then and attempted to turn on her side, but he climbed fully atop the bed and straddled her back and Scarlett's entire backside was open to him. He rested his weight on her shoulder blades and she tensed when the whistle of the swinging belt cut the air and she shrieked with pain as again and again the leather strap met her tender flesh, the sharpness of the sting causing her eyes to bulge and her legs kicked wildly in an attempt to escape the lashing.

After several more burning whips of the belt, Tomas climbed off of the bed and left Scarlett weeping into the pillow beneath her.

"If you ever disobey me again, I'll break your neck."

Scarlett jumped when the metal of the belt buckle struck the ground and all she heard was his heavy breathing as he stormed from the room and Scarlett lay there stunned at her burning skin.

She reached behind her and gingerly ran her hand along the back of her thighs and felt for welts.

She couldn't believe that he had hit her.

!

CHAPTER THREE

Auschwitz-Birkenau

Tomas heard voices and he blinked several times and tried to rush his eyes to adjust to the darkness around him.

Plop. Plop. Plop.

Water. There was water dripping from somewhere nearby and the sound was driving him crazy. All he wanted was just a few drops for the dry tongue that had swelled and now clung to the roof of his mouth. His head felt heavy and was too much weight for his neck to bear. Even the simple act of breathing seemed like too much work in the suffocating hole where he stood. All he wanted to do was lie down, but all he was able to do was stand or squat on aching legs or lean against the wall in what he felt was an upright coffin. There was nowhere else to go. There was no way out.

It was cold, but he was grateful for the chill because he felt hot all over. Sweat trickled from his brow and into his eyes and he turned his head in an effort to steer the wet trail to the corner of his mouth where he forced his tongue out, grateful for the few drops of moisture.

Exhausted, he leaned his head forward and rested his chin on his chest then winced at the feel of sticky, cold vomit that had soaked into the collar of his shirt. As a solid wave of dizziness swept over him, he inhaled a deep breath to fight the darkness that threatened to again take over his consciousness.

Fever...

On shaky legs, Tomas reached down as far as he could and inspected his injured calf then grunted as his fingers slipped into the painful, sticky mess he found there, and Tomas winced as he tried to dislodge the fabric of his pants where they had dried and adhered to his wound. His arm wasn't much better but he was able to move his fingers and eventually his sore arm. But his leg worried him.

He ran a dry tongue over his chapped lips and lay his head back against the wall and tried to recall how he had gotten into his current predicament, and while he probed his aching ribs, he chuckled to himself then flexed his right fist as he recalled how hard the shocked officer had hit the ground. He then remembered Amos' insane laughter.

Amos. He grimaced and gritted his teeth. Where was Amos? Was he lying dead on Koch's property with Major?

Pop. Pop. Pop.

Tomas jumped at the sound then shook his head to clear his disoriented brain. Voices then...pop, pop, pop. Gunshots...laughter...pleading combined with mournful moaning...the shaky, terror-ridden voice of a man praying loudly. Then again in quick succession...pop, pop, pop.

Grief-stricken, Tomas turned and looked up into the darkness and wished for even a thin slit of light to escape into the cell from above his head.

He didn't know how much time had passed. In the first moments when he would awake, he would be startled by the blackness that surrounded him until his memories flooded back to him in a solid rush. Blowing warm breaths into palms enclosed over his mouth gave him comfort, though the silence around him was as still as the dark, and he felt as if he had been thrown into the abyss and forgotten. It was rare that food was thrown into the hole and hunger gnawed at his gut until he felt as if his stomach was eating itself. He stretched his limbs as far as they would go and grunted at the pain in his leg, and as time passed, he counted to himself, scratching his itchy scalp in irritation...

10,001. 10,002. 10,003...

When he lost count, he would recite the commandments out loud until they became a jumble in his head. Gideon. Jakob. Mom...

When he felt that he was going to suffocate, he would go mad and scream in insane rage, beating at the walls around him with numb fists until he collapsed in exhaustion.

Twenty-three days later...

It was dark but there was light. He felt rough hands on him...dragging him and he grunted as his ankle scraped against something sharp - then searing pain and a warm wetness gushing around his foot. He tried to get his feet up under him but faltered weakly, and his naked leg trailed behind him, useless and painful.

He could hear voices...loud...and as he was thrown into a chair he felt as if his head would split from the base of his skull clear to his forehead, and he found that he could not control the intense shaking of his body.

Then there was light...

He shielded his eyes with his hands and ducked, preparing for a blow. His eyes sprang open and he winced at the brightness of light and then blinked rapidly feeling as if ice cold water had been thrown on him. A bulb swung pendulum-like above his head casting the room in bright light then dim shadows and everything before him seemed fuzzy, and Tomas shook his head and tried to clear his dazed mind but the light was blinding and he felt a sense of urgency to see his surroundings and cursed his eyes for being weak to the light.

A buzzing. Deep and low surrounded him and he concentrated on it, trying to find its direction.

Brrrrrr...

Like a hive of bees, the machine-like vibration seemed to surround him. It whirred closer and became soothing, almost lulling, and the voices around him faded into the background, but as his head lolled forward, he snapped awake again when rough hands groped at him yanking his head back - laughing, pulling and then a stinging, tearing sensation on his arm...sharply gliding too deeply over the tender flesh until pain reverberated into his bone.

Scissors, cold and hard ran swiftly over his scalp and itchy hair fell into his eyes and across his bare chest...he was naked. Instinctively, Tomas cupped his genitals as rough hands restrained him and shaved the thick hairs that covered his groin. Raucous laughter again met his ears and reeking, relentless fingers poked at his face and taunted him scornfully about his circumcised penis and Tomas growled and snapped his teeth weakly at the cruel hands and was rewarded by being beat about the head with strong, heavy fists before being thrown to the ground.

Booted feet raced at him and Tomas shielded his body with his arms and squinted as he desperately tried to see the figures that moved toward him.

"I'll take him!"

An urgent voice and strong arms enclosed him and pulled

him to stand on shaky legs and he shrank away from the contact -
dizzy, heart thudding in his chest as the instinct to survive ebbed
and waned inside of him. He knew that he would be dead if he
could see, and as he stood swaying on trembling legs, he blinked
rapidly and held on tight to the arms that impatiently pulled him
along.

"Keep moving!" A hot, harsh voice whispered fiercely in
his ear and Tomas did not argue, but moved along weakly,
sometimes stumbling onto the feet of the man who half-carried him
down the corridor.

"Keep walking."

The harsh voice came to him again and then he found
himself outside in the dim darkness of night and he remembered
that he was naked and again reached a hand out to cover his penis.
His eyes adjusted better to the night and he looked up at the man
who pulled him along – tight faced and bald in the moonlight with
hard lines around his eyes and mouth. Tomas' stomach churned
and he deeply inhaled the cool air in an attempt to ward off a
sudden wave of nausea.

His throat was dry and he tried to clear his throat before speaking. *"What's burning?"*

A flash of painful uncertainty passed across the man's face and he pressed his lips together and continued to drag Tomas across the hard earth and then onto moist, dirt filled terrain.

"Who are you?" Tomas whispered.

After a pause the once harsh voice softened. *"I am Eli."*

Tomas again took a deep breath and frowned. Faint but definite, something was burning and it reminded Tomas of smoked meat, but with a peculiar charred odor that he could not recall smelling before. Again, he looked up at the man who pulled him along, sensing something sadistically evil in the air. He felt as if he were in a night terror and he swiftly turned and surveyed his surroundings.

"What's burning?" He asked again louder almost in a panic.

"It'll be you if you don't shut up and keep moving." Came the urgent reply.

Impatient to question the man further, Tomas opened his

mouth too wide to speak and grimaced as his dry, bottom lip cracked in the corner and he instantly touched the tear with the tip of his tongue as he looked warily about him, squinting into the dark, moon-filled night.

"Halt!"

Tomas stiffened in response to the fear that radiated from Eli's sturdy body. They turned slowly, Tomas naked and shivering, Eli terrified but calm, and waited as the heavily clothed SS guard approached them.

"Where are you going?" He spit ferociously.

"Commander has instructed me to take him."

The man turned and slowly looked Tomas' hunched, shivering figure over from head to toe. "He doesn't look like much."

Eli quickly piped up though his head was lowered. "Yes. But he is strong."

They stood closely side by side and Tomas could feel Eli's heart pounding against his own ribs as they waited. After several painful seconds of staring at the pair with annoyed, thoughtful *contempt, he turned and walked away.*

"There are more pieces to be loaded for the crematoria. Hurry up."

Pieces? What pieces?

Tomas' still dazed mind raced as he was pulled along and just when he thought he could go no further, they stopped in front of a small, brick structure and stepped inside. Men sat around and carelessly eyed him as Eli lowered him onto a musky, straw mattress. Tomas turned his head and watched the unconcerned men – some young like himself, some older – as they ate from bowls and drunk steaming cups of coffee.

Tomas groggily expressed his gratitude as he tried to force his heavy eyelids to remain open. He wanted to ask for something to eat – something to drink, but he couldn't find his voice. The last thing he remembered was Eli's sure fingers moving over him and then deep, black darkness.

Smacking him. Smacking his face.

He lifted his arms and swatted weakly at the playful hands then became somber as his eyes opened and his memories again rushed back.

Amos. Amos was staring down at him – had his hands on either side of Tomas' head to steady himself. He smelled awful and Tomas' face screwed into a deep frown as the smell of smoke wafted up his nostrils. An insane, tortured gleam lit Amos' eyes and Tomas closed his own, knowing that something was deeply wrong – even more wrong than the Warsaw Quarter.

"Welcome to Birkenau!" Amos whispered fiercely down at him.

Tomas opened his eyes again and lifted his head to look down at his now clothed body. Thin, brown pants covered his legs, scuffed black boots, a frayed, yellow shirt and a gray jacket whose sleeves were too short for his long arms. He looked around the dark, dank room where empty cots littered the floor. The walls were stained in spots by rust water and cobwebs clung to the corners of the ceiling.

"It's so warm." Tomas said hoarsely, thinking that his fever had returned.

Amos whispered and moved his head toward Tomas, forcing him to meet his gaze. "Did you see them?"

Tomas did not want to look at Amos or hear his fervent whispering. They had been friends for a long time and he could hear the mourning in Amos' voice. He did not want to talk about it.

"Did you smell them burning?"

Tomas lay his head back on the mattress and again closed his eyes. He felt very tired. "Do you have any food, Amos?"

"Yes, yes."

Under half-closed lids, Tomas watched him scurry across the room to a lone mattress that sat neatly rolled in the corner and reached inside to retrieve two tomatoes and hard bread. He seemed to Tomas to be jittery and panic-stricken. In a crouched crawl, he moved swiftly back to Tomas and handed him the meager fare along with a rusted cup that was partially filled with lukewarm water.

"I saved half for you." Amos whispered and sat back on his haunches, wrapping his arms around his slender legs and rocking slowly forward then backward, his eyes never leaving Tomas' face.

"You were in the hole?"

Tomas nodded as he gulped the water down, choking on the liquid as it made a burning path down his dry throat. He coughed loudly, almost choking, then ignored the pain in his throat and shoved dry bread into his mouth and leaned forward to bite greedily into one of the tomatoes.

"I am told you should thank God that you are alive."

Tomas leveled his gaze on Amos. "They were shooting them outside my cell."

Amos pulled up a dirty sleeve to reveal a row of numbers that had been etched into the flesh of his forearm and eyed him questioningly, and Tomas paused mid-chew and lifted his sleeve to expose his own line of numbers.

"They have put us in hell, Tomas." Amos said weakly and his voice broke.

He sobbed pitifully into his shirt, wiping his tear filled eyes with the ragged hem, and Tomas averted his eyes, feeling sad for his friend.

"They house them in large barracks - several hundred

souls all crammed together in buildings where the vermin run wild, and in the mornings, they awake with the ones that have died in their sleep.

There is no remorse for them - ever. They wake them early in the morning and line them up - Eli says even in the snow with no coats." Amos sighed heavily. "And when they drop dead during roll call, no one bats an eyelash."

Tomas stared down at his bread. "And the skeletons, Amos?"

"Oh, yes. Still here there is hardly any food. The rations are meager – watery soup, moldy bread. Here, you piss when you're told to piss, and if they catch you in the wrong place at the wrong time, you're as good as dead. And they work them…they work them to death. Some jump onto the fence and electrocute themselves…" Amos' voice trailed off.

"What else?" Tomas prodded.

Amos stared shamefully down at his feet. "Pits. They make large graves in the earth and fill them with corpses – hundreds of them buried or burning."

Tomas placed a hand on Amos' shoulder. "And you have seen them?"

"I have filled them." Again, Amos choked back a sob.

Tomas shrunk back, alarmed. "What do you mean?"

Amos looked up with swollen, tear filled eyes. "When we first got here, they put me in the camp with the others for a few days before I came here. Eli said that my time would be easier. I would have food, cigarettes even, so I agreed. I don't know. What was I to do?

They came and got us early the next morning – rode us away from the camp out to one of the buildings, I didn't know where. They were standing out there with the SS, hundreds of them, women, babies, the old. The SS screamed at them, beat them about the body with their fists, kicked them – even the women." Amos stared down at his feet again. "They line them up and tell them that they are going to shower. Sometimes they trick them – give them soap. They tell them, yes, yes. Hang your clothes where you can easily retrieve them...don't forget where your things are. But they lie to them.

Tomas stared at him in disbelief. "And they kill them with gas?" He asked.

Amos nodded. "Some of them know that they are going to die, and they become so afraid, Tomas. They cram them in all together where they can hardly move and when they drop the gas in there's screaming, Tomas. There's so much screaming, but when they open the doors it is silent and they fall over like dead weight. They are covered in vomit and blood. Some are crushed from being trampled during the panic…" Amos sobbed between breaths. "We load the bodies onto carts and take them to the crematoria or burn them in the pits."

"How could you do that, Amos?"

"I didn't know what to do. I was stunned. I didn't want to die. I didn't want to go into the pit."

"I won't do it." Tomas growled and balled his fists. "I'll die on the gate first."

Amos again began his rocking. "You have deeper trouble than that. The officer you hit…"

Tomas stared steadily at his friend, a friend that he had

known many years and now found broken, almost docile, and

Tomas' heart thudded in his chest.

What was this new evil?

"He is the only reason that you are alive. He put you here

for a reason. He wants you to suffer for knocking his eye out."

Tomas' eyebrows rose in surprise. "I thought I broke his

nose."

"No." Amos shook his head. "His right eye is gone. He

wears a patch now. He begs the commander to tell Eli to make you

well, to make you work with the Sonderkommando in the

crematoria, and then eventually he will come for you."

***

He felt as if he were moving in slow motion. He knew he

wouldn't make it to her on time – he knew it, but he continued to

run toward her anyway. The rain had stopped but the earth was

muddy and slowed his progress. He screamed until his throat

burned but there was no one around to hear his cries for help. She

stood there on the train tracks waving. Her ragged, sackcloth dress

was drenched and clung to her body — stretched taught over the large belly that protruded out in front of her. Her hair, damp and stringy, stuck to her wet, gaunt face.

Tomas screamed for her to step away from the tracks, waving his arms wildly and gesturing toward the approaching train. He stopped and again looked wildly about for help but found no one. Even the watchtowers were empty. He turned back and stumbled, falling hard into the mud and scrambled again to his feet. She stood there, still as stone, only moving a hand to wave at him with an empty smiled plastered onto her face. When the train hit her, crushing her body beneath the wheels, Tomas fell to his knees screaming, pounding his head with his fists.

A humming...

Tomas' head snapped up as the rain started again – as dark storm clouds rolled across the sky and thunder cracked...

Miriam...humming the hatikvah.

Tomas fell on his backside and wiped frantically at his eyes with the sleeve of his shirt. A man now stood on the train tracks staring down at the remains of the woman. His black uniform was starched, dry and clean, though he stood under the steady, heavy rainfall. A black beret with a skull medallion attached to its center sat perched perfectly atop his straw-colored hair, and the red band that enclosed his upper arm seemed to burn and glow around the black swastika that sat in its midst. Their eyes met and the Nazi officer threw his right arm into the air in salute. He grinned then, cruel and barbaric, and though it was dark and they were some distance apart, Tomas cringed at the sight of the chunks of flesh that clung to the man's teeth.

And then a deeper humming... Gideon...

Tomas searched the dark - squinted his eyes against the hard rain as his hands sunk into the thick, wet dirt around him. The dark figures of a man and woman approached him in shadow, but he could not make out their faces...

***

"Wake up, Tomas. We must go."

Tomas opened his eyes slowly to a red-eyed, sour-faced Amos staring down at him. "If you want to eat then we have to get to work." He grumbled.

Tomas pulled himself to a sitting position and rubbed his

hands over his sore body to take measure of how much pain still

existed in his limbs. Around him several other men moved about

quickly; some sat pulling on boots while others mechanically

chewed dry bread as they headed from the building.

Once they made their way outside, Tomas followed the lead

of the others – of Amos mostly, who he trailed closely behind. At

the head of the line was Eli, and he walked stiff-backed behind four

grim looking guard who led them in front and to the side of them.

They went some ways before he saw them – wretched,

moving about with dark, unseeing eyes, gaunt with an air of misery

that hovered about them. They stood together under the warm

glare of the early morning sun cowering with bent backs. The long

buildings where they were housed stretched as far as his eyes

could see, and they stared at them as they passed and Tomas

wanted to call out, wanted to raise a hand in greeting, but he

halted, fearful of calling the guards' attention to himself. His heart

broke at the conquered sight of them as they moved about and he

noted how some averted their gaze when he tried to make eye

contact.

"We are considered unclean in the camps," Amos whispered over his shoulder.

Tomas looked down at his feet and fought back frustrated tears of defeat. They were no better than mangy dogs – had been manipulated into turning against one another. He grit his jaw then and wondered what Gideon would say.

Tomas kept his head down as they walked and concentrated on the heel of Amos' boots. To calm himself, he counted his steps and thought of escape. When they finally stopped, Eli left them to speak to another prisoner who was dressed in the garb of the camp – striped outfit and cap – but his dark eyes burned fiercely in his face while he spoke and gestured impatiently with his hands towards a barrack behind him.

"He's a kapo." Amos whispered, seeing Tomas' confusion at the way the man spoke with authority. "They run the barracks."

Other men in striped attire moved in and out of the barrack carrying suitcases and armloads of clothing. Tomas stiffened as Eli approached and then waved them to follow him into the building.

Tomas gasped as they entered, surprised at the mountains

of clothing, shoes and suitcases that greeted them as they walked through the door. He sighed with relief, glad that he had escaped the torturous experience that Amos had recounted to him. Eli set him about sorting men's pants and coats, and to his surprise, gave him a long razor blade with which to cut the fabric to search for valuables that may have been sewn into the lining by the previous owners.

"This is what we call Kanada. We sort the things here," Eli whispered, as was his habit, "and anything of value is sent back to Germany. If you are lucky, you will find food." Eli turned his head slightly to eye an officer who intently watched the men and a few women go through the piles of suitcases, sometimes barking orders in an aggressive tone. "But be careful."

Tomas did not turn to watch Eli depart but began his work, and as the hours passed he became less surprised at the things he found – photos of smiling families that he did not know, gold, currency of all kinds, and most importantly, food. Every item he touched reminded him that these things belonged to actual people and he wondered what their names were - or had been. He wondered if his own things were there somewhere beneath the piles. The mundane task did not take much thought, and eventually Tomas' mind wandered to Warsaw, and he prayed that his father was still alive.

They worked throughout the day and when night fell, they followed Eli from the barracks and into another building where they sat and ate a meal of dry bread and stew.

Amos ate his food slowly, chewing absentmindedly as he stared blankly into space and Tomas did not try to draw him into conversation. Amos had avoided him all day and he wondered what was on his friend's mind. Most of the men around them were the same – blankly staring into space. They chewed with grizzled jaws and looked about aimlessly, their eyes tired and emotionless. Others laughed and joked, animated by the warm food that filled their stomachs, at times catching Amos' attention, and he stared at them resentfully before looking away as if startled, as if something had caught his gaze, and Tomas would turn in the same direction, expecting something unexpected and finding nothing.

"What time do you think it is?"

Surprised by the question, Tomas turned to Amos and frowned then looked around and shrugged his shoulders. "I don't know. Seven, eight maybe."

"I wish I knew." Amos replied longingly.

They moved around the camp, sometimes sleeping in a different place than the night before. Several days passed before Tomas got his first taste of what Amos had spoken to him about. In the mornings when they went out for their work detail he did not lift his head to his surroundings. He came to expect each day to be as demeaning as the day before and usually became lost in thoughts of Gideon and Jakob and hoping that they were surviving the ghetto without him.

This day, he had climbed in and out of the small truck without thinking so that when they stepped into a housing barrack he looked up and choked at the view around him.

Most of the camp residents were off working – subdued into forced labor around the camp, and the bodies that lay on the bunks in the long building were eerily still and Tomas' heart pounded in

his chest as he watched the other men walk over to bunks and lift

frail bodies from the wood.

Women. Some had soiled themselves sometime during the

night and their dresses carried the stench of dried urine.

"Move!"

A male voice screamed at him harshly and Tomas snapped

to attention, telling himself that this was no different than the dead

bodies that he had become accustomed to seeing in the ghetto, and

he got his bearings about him and walked over to a bunk on stiff

legs and stared down at a woman whose open-mouth, wide-eyed

stare stayed with him throughout the day. Her face was fixed in a

grimace of pain and she clutched a stiff hand to her stomach. A

woman. He didn't want to touch her. He hated that her blank eyes

watched him; hated that she depended upon him to move her.

He reached a hand down and used trembling fingers to

close her eyes then took a deep breath and lifted her small, cold

body from the wooden bunk, holding her as far away from him as

he could, not wanting to feel her against him, and carried her

outside where other corpses were heaped upon a handcart where
SS men stood leisurely about with rifle straps slung casually over
their shoulders, conversing as if oblivious to what was happening
around them.

Tomas screamed at his brain and fought a strong urge to
count the dead. He tried to avert his eyes as he placed her atop the
pile of gaped mouth men and women, and though he hated
touching her, he waved his hands over her in a panic, not wanting
any one of the swarming flies to land on her face.

"You had better move!" Eli whispered loudly in his ear and
Tomas jumped and turned, realizing that he was blocking other
men from dispensing of their loads, and he loathed Eli for the
complacent fear in his voice. "You never seen a dead body before?
Move!"

Weeks passed that way, with Tomas going to work in
Kanada after removing corpses from the barracks in the mornings
– corpses of the severely starved who had once moved about the
camp like phantoms, plaintively moaning "jestem glodny" – the

ones whom the other prisoners and SS had nicknamed muselmen.

Amos grew increasingly detached as time passed. He stuck close to Tomas as always, but he rarely spoke, and the best response that Tomas could ever expect was a gruff, humpf or a stiff nod. And Tomas' mind remained always on escape though he knew that his chances were less than slim.

The morning before his mental break – before chaos ensued, Tomas thought that he had finally conquered his brain; that his instinct to survive had taken over and that he would persevere and survive the storm.

He had inhaled the crisp, early morning air. He was glad to be away from the barracks though every now and again there was a bark from a dog or a curse from the Nazis that lined the train tracks, but other than that, there was silence. He turned to look at Amos, and again his gaze was avoided. Amos seemed guilty, sad, and Tomas wondered if he was hiding something.

He saw lights in the distance as a train came barreling down the tracks then the solemn screech and everyone around him came to life. He could feel Eli's eyes upon him – the man watched him like a hawk, and Tomas met his gaze and nodded then smiled

relieved when Eli returned his nod then stuck his chest out and

pointed a finger at him as if indicating for him to be strong. Then

he turned and pointed at the train.

Guards rushed the cattle trucks with crowbars, banging

loudly upon them as they slid the doors open. Tomas' heart

skipped a beat as people flooded the tracks in the hundreds, some

falling to the ground as they were herded out with screams and

stinging blows. The cries of children and shouting Nazis filled the

air. The elderly, unstable on their feet, hit the ground hard and

were pulled up by dazed relatives.

People rushed about in a panicked frenzy, scared, crying –

some tried to ask questions and were beaten back. The kapos

interspersed expertly into the crowd, moving people away from the

tracks to line up in a long procession where officers stood stiffly,

unspeaking, cold and malicious, separating men from their

families. Women wailed, begging not to be separated from their

children and were roughly cursed and shoved to the left, while

other women acquiesced and handed small children over to

relatives with the assurance that they would rejoin them later.

Tomas stared about wide-eyed. There were so many people!

But with cruel eyes, SS men snatched the elderly from the hands of loved ones with the flick of a leather bound hand that decided their fate and either to the left or right they went, some bloody and beaten, in a confused, tired state, but looking forward to the promised shower and meal that was to come.

Tomas stood stupefied, not believing his eyes. Suitcases, plants and items wrapped neatly in white sheets littered the ground, and as Amos and the men moved about with downcast eyes he joined them without being prodded. He moved about in a daze collecting suitcases to be sent to Kanada even though their return had been promised to the people who had carried them. At times his eyes would flit to the train cars where Eli and another group of men removed passengers who had not survived the long journey in the cramped, suffocating confinement.

As the group of people who had been separated to the left were loaded onto trucks with some following on foot surrounded by SS guards, Tomas breathed a sigh of relief when he noticed the white truck that brought up the rear and the red cross that was painted on the side of it.

Eli left some men to continue gathering luggage while he chose others to follow him to a lorry, Tomas and Amos included, and they were driven into a deserted area where the crowd stood among the trees weeping while they were forced to undress and leave their clothing among the bushes – among the bushes near a brick cottage that was conveniently secreted away just beyond a grove of birch trees.

Tomas shook his head as a sense of foreboding overcame him. His stomach churned and he punched his head with his fists to clear his mind. No, he did not like it.

Why were the windows all covered up? Why was this little cottage sitting here all alone?

With trepidation they cried, the women hysterical, clutching their children to them and Tomas could hear their whispers. Their voices mingled together and he held his breath and concentrated, singling out the hushed tones.

"We are going to be gassed!"

"No, we are going to be disinfected. They have said that very clearly. Pay attention."

And others...

"Did you see those boys jumping from the trains?"

"I saw the one that got his foot stuck between the rails. I saw the ones they shot dead."

"Shut up, Anna."

And another, "Finally a shower. I thought I would die in that sweat box."

And a girl his own age – pretty and dark-haired glaring at him from across the clearing through teary eyes and Tomas lowered his gaze, embarrassed for her. He knew her humiliation in having her body bared to strange, leering eyes, but when he looked up again she was gone, and he scanned the crowd for her to no avail as several hundred faces blurred together.

Tomas cringed as the kapos voices met his ears.

"Yes, yes. Here you will undress for your shower...yes, yes, yes. You may keep your child with you...I'm sorry, men and

women do shower together."

Tomas felt as if he were suffocating. He wanted to open his mouth to warn them, but he couldn't find his voice. You're going to be murdered, his mind screamed. He knew it. He wanted to shout it, but even when he said it to himself the words seemed like nonsense.

And then there was the stricken look on Eli's face as he watched Tomas from several feet away. Tomas knew what Eli was thinking, but he ignored him as he watched the Nazis herding the crowd into the small house and he felt panicked. His eyes darted to the cold faces of the SS men and women as they cruelly drove the people and he stepped forward and opened his mouth to yell...

"Tomas." Eli placed a heavy hand on his shoulder then looked warily around. "You and Amos go with Henry and wait, okay?"

Tomas nodded, but still his feet remained planted to the ground. He cleared his throat and tried to find his voice.

Then the harsh whisper, "Even if you yell, they will die. If you tell them, they will panic and run. They will scatter, but still,

314

they will shoot them down." Eli stood in front of Tomas and

blocked his view. "Then we will have to go out and collect them.

That will make our job harder. Do you understand?"

Tomas could not concentrate on Eli's words. There were so

many people. How could they not know, Tomas thought anxiously

and began to pace, still disregarding Eli.

"If you yell, I will make sure that you go out with the work

crews that are digging up the dead." Eli threatened through

clenched teeth.

His fists balled at his sides and his temples pulsated as he

and Tomas glared at one another.

"Yes. They are digging up buried corpses with Jewish

labor and burning them." Eli hissed.

Horrified, Tomas did not speak but his eyes darted back to

the small cottage.

Eli followed his gaze then turned back to him and his soft,

brown eyes pleaded. "There's nothing you can do. Don't terrify

them. Think of the women and children."

A truck pulled up to the house and a tall, masked man

climbed out and moved toward the house carrying a canister that was clearly marked "Poison". Minutes passed before there came a loud beating, as if a vibrating thunder came from beneath the ground.

No, no, no! Tomas' mind screamed in horror and he paced the ground in angst.

And the SS stood about fingering the triggers of rifles and submachine guns watching them with a sadistic gaze - their eyes falling upon them individually as they waited for their reaction - hoping to see their insides crumble.

Like demons, Tomas thought hatefully.

But still they maliciously mocked them with their evil presence. They stood in the midst of dresses, socks, baby clothes...watching, and the smell of fear wafted from Eli in waves. Though his life was miserable he still clung to it. Tomas was feeling indifferent about his own. He could not live like this – would not.

When his eyes again fell upon Eli, the man appeared haggard, as if he had done a day's hard labor in fifteen minutes time, but still he remained stone faced. His eyes again fell upon

Tomas and they held each other's gaze – Eli pleading with the

younger man to remain calm while Tomas calculated the loss in

his mind and decided that he would decide his own fate.

He turned and looked over at Amos who refused to look up

though Tomas knew that he felt his eyes upon him, and as the chill

of the early morning waned and the light of the sun overtook them,

he could see wetness glistening upon Amos' face as he moved

about with the others gathering the discarded items.

Sickening silence prevailed and Tomas' heart ached. He

tensed in anticipation as the kapos removed striped caps to wipe

sweat from their brows, and Tomas followed Eli as the man moved

stealthily among shoes that had been tied at the laces and were

now being gathered and carried away. The stench of murder

fouled the air and Tomas felt indescribable sadness settle over him

like a heavy quilt and Eli's orders to move faster were drowned out

by the heavy thudding of his heart. He wished that he was in a

night terror and he found that sometime during his horrified daze

he had picked up a shirt and he now clutched it in his hands and fingered the collar, searching for comfort.

A stern faced Nazi stood boldly near the door of the cottage and as Eli and Henry approached, the blank-faced SS man pulled the door open and Tomas stumbled backwards and fell to the ground at the nightmarish sight before him.

Human beings stood as still as stone, unmoving, as if frozen – others lay piled haphazardly atop one another. Tomas crawled to his knees still tightly clutching the shirt in his hands. He had watched children go into the small house – babies...

The crew absentmindedly went to work removing the bodies - dragging them from the sawdust covered floor by their limbs and stockpiling them to be taken away towards the large holes that had been dug beforehand – to the open graves that waited nearby.

He saw Amos stop and stare at his gloved hands and grimace. Tomas knew that though it was warm, Amos did not want to remove the cloth that protected his skin - did not want the sticky mess that had accumulated in the fabric to touch his flesh.

Tomas could hear shouting – could feel something hard prodding at him but he was dazed – unable to believe the sight before him. There were so many...

No, he would not go near them.

"Hauptscharfuhrer, what are we running here, a coddling place? Is he a wee one?" A loud voice said above him and Tomas looked up to see a heavyweight man standing over him in the garb of the camp officers. Though he was talking about Tomas, he did not look down at him, but addressed a short, young officer who stood nearby.

"He is okay." Eli's humble voice piped up beside him and Tomas felt his heavy, moist hand rest on his shoulder. Tomas could hear the disapproval in his quiet tone. *"It is his first time...his mind is shocked."*

"Ah." The man replied in a cold tone. *"I thought a retard had somehow made his way into the bunch."*

The officers that stood around did not laugh at the joke of their superior officer, but looked down on Tomas with open contempt while he blinked wildly and shook his head to clear the vision of blank eyes and gaping mouths. He had just heard them speaking and now they were nothing but a mountain of corpses...

319

This was the reason for Amos' docility. The very sight of body after body being stacked and carried away - the knowledge and smell of systematic death surely helped one ease into the transition of submissiveness.

"On your feet."

Tomas grimaced as a hard object was brought down upon his back, but still he did not rise. The next blow made Eli cry out and he hurriedly pulled Tomas to his feet with a curse, only to be knocked to the ground himself. "They" snatched him up then, two of them, and turned him to face the fiendish looking commander.

Tomas looked him squarely in the eye, unflinching even when he smiled and removed his pistol and calmly placed the barrel against Tomas' heart, and the men paused in their removal of the dead to watch the exchange. Tomas heart beat painfully, but slowly, and he stooped humbly, his eyes leveled on the man, and placed an index finger beneath the barrel of the gun and slowly lifted it until it rested in the center of his forehead and the commander let out a whispered, "Ah..."

"Squeeze it." Tomas said, his voice wrought with emotion

but steady.

The smell of burning flesh filled the air and he remembered that there had been voices while he slumbered. He had been half-asleep, falling into a dream, but he remembered well what they said. Their voices beat his brain like a drum...

"He wants the holes dug in a way where the fat drains from the bodies as they burn."

"The fat?"

"Yes, to be used to keep the fire burning..."

The commander hesitated with his mouth slightly open, watching Tomas with an amused expression on his face.

"Do it!" Tomas screamed.

Thick, gray smoke billowed and swirled – heavy clouds of it trailing skyward and the smell was driving him insane. He lunged for the man, wrapping his strong hands around the commander's thick throat until his face turned red and his eyeballs bulged from his head. He heard the gunshot but he felt no pain, so intent was he on crushing the man's windpipe, and he refused to let go of his prize even after heavy boots and fists descended upon his body and head, but still with a strangled roar he persisted, determined to extract his pound of flesh, and growled with satisfaction as he settled his mouth over the bewildered man's nose and shredded his face with his teeth.

He was stretched taut, twirling in the middle of the room, suspended by his arms from chains that hung from the ceiling. Again he was naked and blood flowed freely from his head where a bullet had grazed his temple. He looked down at himself and became startled at the stream of blood that ran down his body and pooled on the floor beneath him.

Groggy, head pounding with pain, blood blurring his vision, Tomas allowed his head to fall back and frustrated tears mingled with his blood. He remembered the beating that he had taken and his shoulders throbbed with a burning pain that extended into his elbows and up into his neck and he wanted to grab ahold of the chain and pull himself up to relieve the agony in his shoulder blades, but he could not feel his fingers.

He remembered then the bodies piled one atop the other

and he swallowed a sob...but then the tortured screams of the commander rang in his ears and he flexed his sore jaw muscles and smiled to himself.

Oh, Tomas, he thought, you've done it now.

He had been a troubled youth – a troubled young man even – but he had thought himself invincible. Nothing had prepared him for what he now faced. "They" would be back and he tried to mentally compose himself for their arrival, knowing that they meant to do him irreparable harm. He could see no other reason for them to keep him alive.

There they were...the heavy fall of sure, booted feet. The guttural sound of their language. The viciousness of their tone.

Tomas whispered the same prayer that he had when he was a youth during the times when the police would march him through the station to an irate Gideon.

They entered – three of them. The bandaged commander gave him a friendly nod and Tomas' heart pounded as a dark-haired man wearing an eyepatch followed closely behind him provoking two barking german shepherds to snarl at him. Tomas' eyes fell to his feet to gauge how far they swung from the ground.

You will not have fear, he told his heart. You will die like a man.

And they whispered...

They whispered urgently and the commander issued a soft, "Ahhh!"

Then even the animals were silent. They whispered with their backs to him and when they turned, their wicked eyes fell straight upon him. He sighed, knowing that their scheming minds would opt first for demonic devices.

He waited. He did not know what they had planned but a fiery fury burned in his stomach. Hatred hung thick in the room as the men eyed one another and Tomas, growing impatient, raised his eyebrows questioningly.

"You're a tough Yid. I know." The commander said softly, dreamily.

Tomas preferred anger, had expected it, but the commander seemed oddly serene as he addressed him. And Tomas became infuriated that the man had power over him and an

324

involuntary groan left his throat, and as they laughed, he struggled

against the chains that held him, the pain in his body forgotten.

"But I know what you're afraid of." The commander

whispered this softly, thoughtfully as he stared up at him with a

mesmerized look in his eyes.

"Let me down." Tomas growled.

He had never expected that they would obey, but to his

surprise they did, and as he went crashing to the ground his heart

jolted and he fell hard, hitting his head – then they let the dogs go,

and finally, he screamed.

He was cold, so cold. His eyes were stuck together – no,

they were glued. He fought to open them but a heavy weight held

his lids down – held him down. He felt pain but the sharp sting that

radiated through his body was not overwhelming. What he

couldn't take was the blindness combined with the restrictive

weight that covered him. He couldn't move – he could hardly

move.

Black. Everything was black and a rotten stench

surrounded him. He felt as if he was falling into one of his night terrors – a dream that started bad from the beginning and so he would fight the heaviness of sleep, fight to open his eyelids. Then relief was his when he escaped the terror immediately before unconsciousness overwhelmed him and he was forced to remain paralyzed with fear - to endure until the night terror ended.

This was different. Yes, he was fully awake. He knew this because he could distinguish sensation from sound. He could smell something rotten. Though something firm and heavy lay upon him, he was able to move his arms until he felt the slide of his fingers across his chest.

A hoarse, tortured groan escaped him and hot tears flowed from his eyes and disappeared against the heaviness, making a slick, cold space between himself and it.

Panicked, he gasped for air then lost control and fought and struggled to free himself, screaming in terrified revulsion as realization assaulted him. His breathing came in short, hard bursts and he became nauseous. He fought them to turn his head, but not before vomit erupted from his throat and into the small space *where not even enough pungent air entered for him to breathe.*

They were all over him... he was buried beneath them... their skin lying against his skin under and atop him. He couldn't breathe and a strangled scream escaped his throat. Like wood. They were like wood.

Then the memory of tufts of huge black and gray smoke trailing its way to the sky invaded his brain and he panicked anew. He had the premonition that he was to be burned alive and terror overtook his mind and he fought like a madman, lifting the bodies from him, weakly pushing with almost useless hands and legs - squirming, crying as he wrenched himself loose a little at a time. When he grew exhausted he rested, his chest rising and falling with an exertion that threatened to overpower him.

Relief flooded him. He could see the sky. It was almost morning, and he could hear birds chirping a song so beautiful that he knew they didn't realize that a massacre was going on all around them. Bloody with crazed eyes, Tomas heaved himself from the grave panting strongly more with fear then exhaustion. There were hundreds...

They were whispering...

Tomas fell over when he heard them and he crouched defensively, but when he tried to rest his weight on his arms he tumbled and his face hit the ground.

"Tomas."

Amos. He turned and there he was...Amos. Standing before him with a haunted look in his eyes. He was afraid. But they were there behind him. Whispering...

A gunshot cracked through the air and he ducked as a bullet hit the ground near his head and he tumbled again and his battered body fell back into the grave. With numb hands, Tomas tried again to scurry from the hole, hardly feeling the rip of his fingernails as he desperately grasped the earth.

Again, their demonic whispering. "Burn him."

He heard them as clear as day. He smelled the gasoline as it was splattered over him - over his head, across his abdomen and onto the bodies surrounding him and he tried again to escape only to be kicked in the face to choke on another warm gush of blood. Tomas stared at his hands in horror. There was so much blood.

"Burn him."

Amos standing with a hunched back, sobbing with a pistol aimed at the back of his head and a matchbox in his hand.

"Burn him now!" The commander screamed, enraged, his face red under the slowly rising sun.

Their eyes met and Tomas watched Amos' heart break. Seconds passed and Amos nodded to him, resolute, and dropped the box to the ground.

"Shoot him!" The commander screamed at the officer behind Amos. "Shoot him now."

"Wait!"

They all turned and stared at the approaching Nazi in surprise, and as he neared, his fellow officers stood at attention saluting him though he did not acknowledge them. His eyes rested steadily upon Tomas. He walked over to Amos and pressed a heavy hand on his shoulder until the young man fell to his knees before him. Then he knelt and picked up the small matchbox and approached Tomas. Their eyes met and agonizing, silent seconds passed as he slid the box open and removed a match stick, holding it up to his face making sure that Tomas' eyes rested intently on its red tip. Tomas closed his eyes and he felt hot all over though cold sweat ran from his pores.

When his eyes again fluttered open, the man from his nightmare remained before him, observing him thoughtfully - then he smiled. He cocked his head at Tomas, beckoning him to crawl from the hole, and he did, scurrying away as he heard the match strike and then heat on his back as the pit went up in flames.

"Polizei." He pointed to himself, trying to communicate with Tomas. "General."

Tomas watched him suspiciously through swollen eyes. This Nazi was unlike any that he had encountered. He was a young man, forty maybe, with neatly sheared blonde hair and intelligent, blue eyes. His nose was long and aquiline, his lips thin and firm over straight, white teeth. He was handsome and amiable, gave off an air of authority and goodwill, but Tomas saw in his eyes a base depravity that sat quietly; that was not loud because it was inevitable. His eyes burned brightly as he spoke, happily even, and

Tomas ceased to check the window beyond his head, but kept his

eyes upon him – wondering at his calm.

They sat in an empty office together in a small building. It

was neat, clean smelling, and unlike what he had become

accustomed to. Behind the general stood a small, square window

and through the curtainless pane he could see Amos outside

kneeling on his knees facing them. The guards around him paced

the ground restlessly, still upset that their fun had been cut short.

"Yusef, right?"

Tomas pulled the thin, tattered gray blanket around his

shoulders the best he could with his battered hands and stared at

the general, unsure of how to answer.

What now? Back to the cell? The dark, dank, pissy smelling

hole where he had almost suffocated...

The general sat back in his seat and crossed his legs and

the high gloss shine of his boots made Tomas want to cry. Why?

He did not know. And he suddenly felt silly...like a woman.

The general chuckled loudly as if something extremely

funny had suddenly occurred to him and he leaned forward and crossed his arms, assessing Tomas curiously.

"We are brothers, you and I."

The general said this with all seriousness, conspiratorially and then winked, snorting at the comedy of his words. And Tomas turned and gazed longingly at the door thinking the man was most certainly mad.

"It is too bad that you were never married, Tomas."

Tomas jumped as the general lifted his hands and clapped them loudly in his face and he turned and gave the man his full attention. The friendliness had left his light eyes and he stared at Tomas in silent warning, and then as quick as it had come, the danger was gone, and he smiled brightly again as if Tomas' company satisfied him immensely.

"I have a beautiful wife." The general said all of a sudden. "I have a son as well." He paused then and rubbed a rough hand over his chin as if unsure of how to proceed. "I met her here in Poland...you know how the war was..." He shrugged his shoulders nonchalantly as if he felt he needed to explain something. "Anyway, long story short, I wanted her. She was a little *spitfire...." The general licked his lips and his eyes took on a*

faraway, unfocused gaze as he reminisced. "She wouldn't have me,

and I couldn't bring myself to force her, so I tricked her instead."

He laughed again then as if he thought himself brilliant. "Tricked

her onto the other side of the wall and threatened to have her shot

for trying to escape."

The other side of the wall?

"She came willingly then. Mmm." The general took a deep

breath then let it out in a long, satisfying sigh. "But then came the

baby. My child. Not a dog."

The general rubbed a large, freckled hand over his face

and sat forward in his seat, resting his elbows upon his knees.

"Anyway, she says to me, Otto, if you do this one thing I

will forgive you for everything else – do this one thing and I will

stay with you forever."

Again the look of dark danger and a finger pointed at him

in warning...

"I tried for your uncle and your parents, but it was too late.

Jakob and your father were deported to Treblinka and gassed just a few days ago. I don't know where your mother is."

Tomas sat with his hands in his lap and tears flooded his eyes. Just a few days...but he had just been with them in Warsaw. It had not been that long ago, had it?

He was suddenly so tired. He stared around the room in a daze and continually tried to swallow the pain that exploded in his chest.

"Where is Avigail?" He asked when he was able to control the tremor in his voice.

"Emma is at home with our son Walter." Again, the dark look of warning and the general's voice took on a distrustful tone. "And if you breathe one word about this, I will burn you alive myself."

Tomas was aware of the floor where his bare, moist feet clung to the ground – of the musty smell of the scratchy, paper thin blanket that draped his shoulders and back. The warmth of the room was almost stifling but awesome sound buzzed in his ears. His sadness was replaced with joy. Avigail was alive.

The general stood outside for some time talking to the now stern-faced commander who angrily shouted orders to the guards around him. Tomas stood in front of the building, filthy and tormented, oblivious to the blanket being lifted from his naked body by warm gusts of wind.

Amos remained on his knees with his head lowered and rocked and hummed quietly to himself, and though Tomas knew that he could feel his eyes upon him, Amos did not look up.

They sent him to the infirmary to have his wounds stitched and cleaned. He awoke in a room by himself on a clean, down-filled mattress covered with fresh, white linen. They had even brought him food, and though his stomach growled at the smell of roasted potatoes and buttered biscuits, he refused to eat – disgusted that people outside were starving while inside this building the air was cleaner and plates were heaped high with delicious food. His clothes were now clean and his boots fit, and he wanted to cry as he wiggled his toes knowing that his feet were covered in clean socks.

The following morning when they came for him, he

panicked and became paranoid that they would murder him. Onto

a small truck he climbed, clumsy with his bandaged hands.

Everything for him seemed surreal and as the truck approached

the gate, he bent his head, still refusing to hope.

Amos. There walking in line behind Eli the same as any

other day. Sorrow clung to Tomas because he could not help Amos

- though he had surely tried. The crew stopped and stared at him

with open-mouthed surprise as he passed. They watched as he was

escorted through the gates to the waiting car of the general.

He did not know his own fate, but he climbed into the

waiting vehicle nonetheless, and as they pulled away from the gate,

Tomas did not look back for Amos, though he felt as if his heart

had exploded and all that remained was a gigantic, bleeding hole.

He had blindfolded him once they were out of sight of the

watchtowers. He handcuffed him in the backseat, and though

Tomas worried, he did not fight. He was resigned to his fate,

whatever it was, and a new calm settled over him. He could hear the general whistling jovially from the front seat, his fingers tapping the steering wheel as he hummed his own tune. Solemnly, Tomas raised his head and thankfully breathed in the fragrant, warm air. The slapping of the tires on the pavement beneath them was calming and he counted the faint taps in his head...

878, 879, 880...

Tears sprang to his eyes again and his throat swelled painfully as he thought of Gideon and Jakob...of Miriam and Major...

But as the morning sun shone brightly in the sky, he basked in the intensity of its warmth. And though sorrow washed over him in waves, relief was there as well, paired with utter joy at the knowing that Avigail was alive – no matter her condition. He did not know what to expect and wished that he could see the general's eyes, but he dared not try to dislodge the cloth that had been wrapped securely about his head.

His body was stiff, pained from bite wounds where his skin had been torn by fangs and then sewn back together again. His nose was surely broken and his eyes were swollen, but he was *grateful to have his sight. Tomas lay his head back and prayed that the general kept his word.*

And just like that, she was there. They sat together in the backseat of the general's car in an empty, dilapidated barn that sat on abandoned property on the outskirts of the countryside. When they had turned off the road and into the dark barn, Tomas had thought himself dead for sure – had thought that the general would not bother to remove the blindfold and would simply turn and shoot him in the face. Instead he had pulled the tight cloth from Tomas' face then slowly, almost hesitantly, opened the door and exited the car. He had left the barn then and several seconds later she had appeared. He knew it was her right away – the way she held her shoulders back and her chin up. Avigail.

He noticed the differences in her as well. She had erased anything of herself that was Yusef and her hair was now blonde and plaited, pinned neatly to her head.

They sat and cried together for a long time – neither speaking, never touching.

"What's happened to you, Avi?"

He whispered this through strangled sobs, through the aching pain in his chest. He would never forget how she had smiled at him, her cheeks rosy and plump - her German accent flawless.

"I have been Germanised as they say."

Tomas shook his head in quiet disapproval. "If Uncle Jakob wasn't dead already, you would surely kill him with this."

Her countenance grew serious then, and she briskly wiped tears from her face with the back of one hand and a grim expression settled on her pretty face. "Our family is dead, Tomas. I have left that life behind."

Tomas stared down at his bandaged hands where they rested in his lap and allowed the familiar feeling of despair to settle over him. "Do you know what's happening, Avi? Do you know what they are doing – what your husband is doing?"

Her head jerked up and she stared at him angrily. Rage bit at her words. "What am I to do, Tomas? Do you think I enjoy hearing them sit around my dinner table discussing their precious

Hitler? Do you?"

She had become hysterical and Tomas settled back in his seat and smiled. He was glad to see that a remnant of his Avigail remained.

"Do you love him?" He asked once she had calmed and her breathing slowed.

"I will when I have proof that you're safe. I will."

Then she hugged him. He had thought that she didn't want to touch him – that he shouldn't touch her. They embraced one another and did not let go. They spoke as they held on, neither wanting to part.

And they whispered...

"Papa is dead." She said through broken sobs and while her shoulders quaked he held her as tightly as he could, ignoring the pain in his body. She pulled back suddenly until they were eye to eye, their faces barely inches apart, and grasped his chin with one hand. "Do you know what happened to Ma-Ma?"

Tomas lowered his gaze then. "She jumped from a window. It was my fault. I was supposed to be watching her –"

And suddenly he felt dizzy – dizzy and nauseous at the memory of Miriam lying twisted and broken in the courtyard. As if she had the same image in her mind, Avigail rocked to and fro, grasping her heart until no sound escaped from her. Tomas released her and waited – waited for her pain to subside. Waited for her to remember to breathe.

"Shhh." He rubbed her hair with his fingertips to comfort her. "Shhh, Avi..."

No longer did they speak. They sat together in the back seat, her with her head resting against his chest and him with a protective arm draped over her as she leaned into the cusp of his arm. She reached into her pocket and pulled a heavy, white envelope from beneath the thick, plaid folds of her skirt and pressed it into his hand.

An hour passed before the general returned.

"How can I part from you, Tomas?" She asked through red, swollen eyes while grasping his collar between strong, pale fists.

And she caressed his face tenderly with her palms,

memorizing every line, the slant of his cheekbones, the prominence

of his brow, the pain in his eyes.

"I love you, Avi." He whispered.

Avigail squared her shoulders then raised her chin with the

strong-willed defiance that stirred in all Yusef blood.

"Do not be soft with the world, Tomas, because the world

will not be soft with you."

***

"Are you shitting me?" Amos sat back in his chair and

stared at Tomas in disbelief while puffing obstinately at his

cigarette.

Annoyed, Tomas shook his head and leaned onto the wall

from where he stood underneath a brass, antique clock.

"How did you get out, Amos?"

"I never really did." Amos replied spitefully. Then, "I

survived until we were liberated. Commander always meant to get

rid of me but never really got around to it." He paused and leveled

a hard gaze on Tomas. "I guess some of us were stronger than

others."

Tomas stared down at his feet and sighed heavily. "We'll never be like we were, eh?"

Still regarding him with a steely glare, Amos slowly shook his head. "Doubt it."

Tomas smirked and returned his cold stare. "It's not my fault I got out!"

"You know, you're right." Amos narrowed his eyes and shook an accusing finger at him. "Your sister was the traitor. All you did was reap the benefits."

Tomas cut his eyes skyward and exhaled in frustration.

"And then you have the nerve to stand here and tell me your little story." Amos sat back in his seat and eyed Tomas.

"We deserved to be there – you and me."

Amos guffawed in shocked surprise. "I didn't."

Tomas laughed out loud with spite and pointed a finger between himself and Amos. "We did. The others didn't but we definitely did."

"We were kids." Amos waved a hand dismissively.

"No, no." Tomas pulled a metal folding chair from its

place where it leaned against a wall and sat across from Amos. "Even before the ghetto, Amos - even before "they" came."

"It's a cold, cold world, Tomas. Besides, I never hurt anybody that wouldn't have hurt me first." Amos shrugged nonchalantly and gave Tomas a conspiratorial wink. "You know that."

Tomas did not respond right away. Instead he allowed the silence to hang between them – allowed it to speak to Amos of how full of shit he was. "Tell me what happened after I left."

"What do you mean what happened?" Amos eyed him with open distaste. "The trains kept coming; they kept gassing them. End of story."

"And what about you, Amos?"

"Me? Off to the crematorium I went." He held his hand several feet off the ground. "After Eli yanked the gold from their teeth, we would pile them this high all around."

With a look of disgust on his face, Amos threw his cigarette butt to the floor and stumped on it. His shoulders rose and fell as he struggled to control his breathing and small beads of sweat rolled down his temples. He balled his fists, clenching and unclenching them on his knees. "I am not alive."

"I was not either – for a long time."

"Because of the camp?" Amos asked hesitantly as if unsure of himself.

"My family, Major." Tomas paused as a wave of insecurity washed over him. "And you."

Amos stared at him a long time without speaking. "I was so angry at you for – " Amos' voice broke and he paused. "For leaving me alone."

Tomas looked down at his feet and exhaled a pained, relieved breath then took advantage of Amos' vulnerability. Maybe he could save his friendship after all.

"I am here now, Amos."

CHAPTER FOUR

Aside from their breathing, silence prevailed in the coolness of the large bedroom. Amir sat at the edge of the mattress with his back to his wife while she leaned against the oak headboard propped up by two pillows – her own and Amir's.

"I remember Amos from when I was a kid." Amir said thoughtfully, almost awe-like. "He hung himself when I was ten. I remember after his funeral that my dad disappeared for weeks. Drove my mother crazy. She couldn't find him anywhere."

"What about your aunt?"

"I spoke to her on the phone once a long time ago – very briefly. She would call every blue moon to speak to dad."

"I can't believe that he never told you about any of this."

"No – I mean, I knew. I just didn't know everything." Amir fell silent for a moment then held the diary up into mid-air and stared questioningly at it. "I wonder what would make my mother do this."

"Maybe you should give it to him, Amir."

A low whistle escaped his lips. "He'll know that I read it. I never could lie to him."

"Then confess, Amir." Ava threw the sheets away and moved her heavy body down the bed towards him. "Tell him everything." She wrapped her arms around his shoulders and placed a warm kiss to the nape of his neck.

"Nah. I don't know about that." Amir said skeptically then chuckled. "Let me think about it for a while."

Ava placed another kiss in the hollow of his throat. "Either way, we may as well finish it."

Amir thumbed through the last remaining pages and nodded somberly then cleared his throat. Ava waited for him to start then looked up to find him scanning the pages. He sat the book down upon the bed and left the room without a word. Ava shrugged and propped the book upon her belly and after several seconds wore a sheepish grin...

***

Hours later when she finally did leave the bed, Scarlett did so carefully, sliding on her soft belly until her feet found the floor then she limped to the closet and donned a robe. The house was quiet again but she knew that Tomas was still home, and she cautiously made her way across the dark hallway. She couldn't hear him moving about but she knew that he was there.

She grimaced as her sore buttocks brushed against the soft fabric of her robe and she mentally kicked herself. She was no longer upset with Tomas. She just didn't know how to fix her error. The thought that he no longer trusted her was unbearable.

Scarlett crept to the door of the spare bedroom and listened then bit her lip as she inched the door open and peeked inside. Tomas stood in front of the terrace doors with his arms folded.

"Don't you ever do that again, Scarlett." He said this as she stepped inside and shut the door behind her.

"I promise."

When he turned and looked at her there was no softness in his eyes. The love that she had been accustomed to seeing there was gone and Scarlett desperately wanted to know what she had to do to make him tender to her again.

Wanting to please him, Scarlett walked slowly towards him, her eyes intent on his face. She untied her robe and let it fall to the *ground, and though his eyes did not soften, there was interest in them, so she turned to the bed and lay upon her stomach.*

She watched him as he removed his pants and then moved to the foot of the bed to stare down at her and she shivered as the weight of his body came down over her. Scarlett turned her head and looked across the room to watch him in the long mirror of the closet door and moaned when his firm, warm mouth pressed gently into the flesh of her tender backside and then her back arched when his tongue swirled and dipped into the crease of her buttocks and up her spine to linger at the nape of her neck.

Her nipples hardened in response and she watched him spread his body over her own and her eyes closed when the heavy hardness of him pressed into her. His mouth trailed hot kisses across her shoulder blades and she watched him in the mirror through half-closed eyes – the fine, bristly hair that covered his body, the muscular curve of his back as he sought entry to her private places and then the lustful way that his body tensed once he found his way inside of her.

Scarlett arched her back and pressed her buttocks into him and groaned in response as he passionately stroked the secret,

pleasurous nerves within her and she became even more aroused

as the mirror displayed his strong body thrusting into her - tense,

muscles taut with bliss as her moist body caressed him.

Scarlett pressed her stomach and hips into the mattress and

closed her legs, tightening her body around him and Tomas

groaned, sliding deeper inside of her as the first orgasm ripped

through her and he wrapped his arms around her and hugged her

to him as their hips continued their feverish thrusts, and Scarlett

watched Tomas' reflection as his hand slid beneath them and

gently cupped her moist mound while the other cradled her face

and when the second orgasm tore through her, Tomas joined her

and they shuddered together in blind rapture…

They lay there together in the cool, brightly lit room and

Tomas held her tightly to him.

"I love you, Tomas."

"Not now, Scarlett."

Tomas turned over onto his side and Scarlett turned with

him and rested her chin on his shoulder, pressing her naked body into his own until he groaned as she knew he would. She leisurely rubbed a hand up his arm and then back down again and slowly, gently, traced the tattooed row of numbers on his forearm with her fingertips then lifted her head and placed a kiss to his back.

Tomas released a hard, quivering pent up breath and Scarlett blinked with surprise when she heard the raw emotion there. "I'm so tired, Scarlett. I haven't been this tired in a very long time."

Scarlett wrapped her arms around Tomas and pulled him to her, and when he turned and rested his head against her breasts, Scarlett placed a kiss on his forehead.

"Why do you hate yourself for surviving, Tomas?"
***

Detroit, 1959

They rode happily through the Motown streets in Scarlett's brand new, sky blue Cadillac. She sat in the backseat with a grinning Amir and listened as Tomas cheerfully chatted from the front seat. He cranked the radio up as the car sped down the road and snapped his fingers, joyfully whistling as he drove. Scarlett leaned back against the leather seat and tapped her foot to the rhythm of the deep baritone that flooded the car, glad that her husband's mood had improved. They sung out happily together...

> *"I got a woman*
> *Way over town*
> *That's good to me...oh yeah!"*

EPILOGUE

"Thanks for helping me clean out the attic, Dad."

Tomas dusted his hands off on his jeans and answered without turning. "No, problem, boy. Glad to help."

Amir's heart pounded in his chest as he waited while his father sorted through two large boxes that sat in the dusty corner of the attic.

"What about this?" Tomas called out suddenly, and lifted a brown, leather book above his head while he continued to rummage through the box.

"What is it?" Amir asked innocently, trying to keep the tremor from his voice.

Tomas sighed and stood, turning the book over then opening it. "Well, it looks like…" His voice trailed off and he stood erect as his fingers moved through the pages then he closed the book and surveyed the cover.

Amir cursed under his breath when he remembered the

353

broken lock that had held the book closed and he quickly turned back to his task of cutting boxes, hoping that the hour they had spent in the attic before coming across the journal had been convincing enough to make his father think he knew nothing about it.

Amir looked over his shoulder and chanced a glance at his father from the corner of his eye. Tomas stared at the book wearily and exhaled, shaking his head in disbelief. He was agitated.

"How much did you read?'

Shit…

Amir felt guilty as sin but he could not lie. "All of it."

Tomas' eyebrows rose in surprise and to Amir's relief, he smiled.

"Are you upset, Dad."

Tomas pushed up his sleeves and gently ran a hand over the pages then shook his head. "No. Though I do wish that you would have said something sooner." He looked up then. "Where'd you find it?"

"Ava found it in the basement."

A frown furrowed Tomas brow. "The basement, you say?"

"Yeah." Amir took a seat on a nearby crate. "Mom died before we bought this house - before we left Detroit even. I don't know how it got here."

Tomas grinned broadly. "I'll bet she put it in with your things."

Amir paused then took a deep breath and asked boldly, "Dad, how'd you survive when you got to America?"

"Well, after the general had me smuggled into the States, I wandered around for a while. I couldn't speak English. I didn't know where I was. I had money though. Your Aunt Avigail made sure of that.

I found a synagogue within the first few days that I was here, and once they heard what I had been through, they were glad to help me find my way. When I no longer had to look over my shoulder, I didn't have a care in the world.

Food. Food was the problem. There was food everywhere and I ate until I was sick." Tomas chuckled loudly and shook his head. "How simple things like eating and being clean are so often taken for granted…"

Amir started to ask his father about Adam Meyer and Benyamin, but decided against it, not wanting to ruin his mood.

Tomas grinned happily at Amir. "So enough of this ruse," he said in his usual matter-of-fact way. "How about a beer?"

Amir returned his smile. "Sure, Dad."

***

Tomas sat on his back porch in an old wicker chair in the dark. He had purchased this property when he left Detroit after Scarlett died. Amir and Ava had wanted him closer to them, and he had been tired of waking up without his wife, so he left the home that they had shared together and moved to New York.

He sat now in the darkness and stared out at the trees that surrounded him - at the glowing eyes that stared out at him from the forest. The night was warm and muggy and the wind was still. He rocked in the chair in the still of night. The embers from the burning tobacco in his pipe glowed red hot in the darkness. The journal sat heavily in his lap and he swallowed hard against the lump that had settled in his throat.

He saw her as clear as the day she had come to the restaurant searching for him. Shy and lovely with bright, brown eyes and a mass of silken, dark curls.

How he had loved her. Oh, how he missed her.

And he whispered to her, knowing that she would shake her head at his words and laugh…

"*Ty jestes kopalni*, my love. You are mine."

www.ingramcontent.com/pod-product-compliance
Lightning Source LLC
Chambersburg PA
CBHW070637180626
46817CB00006B/2154